Vilhelm's Room

TOVE DITLEVSEN

Vilhelm's Room

Translated by Sophia Hersi Smith and Jennifer Russell

PENGUIN BOOKS

PENGUIN CLASSICS

UK | USA | Canada | Ireland | Australia
India | New Zealand | South Africa

Penguin Classics is part of the Penguin Random House group of companies whose addresses can be found at global.penguinrandomhouse.com.

Penguin Random House UK
One Embassy Gardens, 8 Viaduct Gardens, London SW11 7BW

penguin.co.uk

Vilhelms værelse first published in Danish in 1975.
This translation first published in Great Britain in 2025.
001

Vilhelms værelse © Tove Ditlevsen & Gyldendal, Copenhagen 1975
Published by agreement with Guldendal Group Agency
Translation copyright © Sophia Hersi Smith and Jennifer Russell, 2025
The translation of Catullus on p. 105 is by A. S. Kline, copyright © 2001

The moral rights of the author and translator have been asserted

Penguin Random House values and supports copyright.
Copyright fuels creativity, encourages diverse voices, promotes freedom of expression and supports a vibrant culture. Thank you for purchasing an authorized edition of this book and for respecting intellectual property laws by not reproducing, scanning or distributing any part of it by any means without permission. You are supporting authors and enabling Penguin Random House to continue to publish books for everyone.
No part of this book may be used or reproduced in any manner for the purpose of training artificial intelligence technologies or systems. In accordance with Article 4(3) of the DSM Directive 2019/790, Penguin Random House expressly reserves this work from the text and data mining exception.

Set in 11.25/14 pt Dante MT Std
Typeset by Six Red Marbles UK, Thetford, Norfolk
Printed and bound in Great Britain by Clays Ltd, Elcograf S.p.A.

The authorized representative in the EEA is Penguin Random House Ireland, Morrison Chambers, 32 Nassau Street, Dublin D02 YH68

A CIP catalogue record for this book is available from the British Library

ISBN: 978–0–241–62898–0

Penguin Random House is committed to a sustainable future for our business, our readers and our planet. This book is made from Forest Stewardship Council® certified paper.

Vilhelm's Room

I

The room is no longer there. Day after day, I saw the destruction progress behind grimy windows as I walked past with no other purpose. I would stand on the Boulevard and peer in at the white destroyers who always pretended not to notice me. Yet there existed between us a strange and fierce understanding, like in the embrace of two people who loathe one another. As I stood in the bright sunlight with my nose pressed to the windowpane, they were seized by a kind of frenzy that seemed to give them superhuman strength. They tore down the walls, lugged the white French doors out on their bare, sweating backs and tossed them into the skip outside the building. They tore up the floors with exaggerated, balletic movements: those small blocks of parquet were not as heavy as they made them out to be. Only when the high, ornate ceilings with the chubby stucco cherubs had disappeared did I lose interest in the wreckage and begin to rebuild the room inside my head. And there it lives now, fraught with whispering shadows, soft laughter like the mocking cries of birds and hot tears kissed away or allowed to flow undisturbed, the way dampness seeps through wallpaper stained with passion and despair. I want to write a book about Vilhelm's room and the events which took place in it, or arose from it; those that led to Lise's death, which I have survived only so that I might write down the story of her and Vilhelm. There is no other meaning to my life. The boy is at a boarding school his father sent him to when he suffered a breakdown after losing his mother. There he's doing reasonably well. Every weekend he is visited by the girl, Lene, who looks like his mother when she was young, and they always talk about his childhood, which is grim and thrilling like a fairy tale, and Lene finds her own childhood so dull in comparison she never mentions it. As for me, I am alone, and all that I do is determined from within. Other people pass straight through me as through a shadow; only a few understand me like the destroyers did, and they too tactfully pretend not to notice me.

I'm residing in a flat two doors down from the old one; I will never truly live here. The word 'home' has lost its meaning, it is simply something I once had. I'm sitting at my typewriter, which these days seems to dictate which keys to press. Otherwise, there is nothing in this unfamiliar room apart from my bed, a wardrobe and a dresser. The window faces a small courtyard with rubbish bins and bicycle racks, just like the courtyard of my childhood. The other three rooms are still full of cardboard boxes, but the widower has left behind the drapes and blinds, as they would not have suited the flat the union obtained for him when the negotiators finally saw an opportunity to store their computer systems in what was once Vilhelm's room. Obviously, it had to be demolished, and the negotiators with their dumb, moist eyes were, just like the destroyers and me, merely a pretext for getting at the inner truth that renders every human life meaningful and interesting. In Lise and Vilhelm's story, which may prove to be about a great deal of things, nothing is accidental, nor could it be any other way. Most facts are irrelevant, but a few suddenly prove to have surprising significance, like fishing out the precise scrap of fabric from the ragbag that brings the pattern to life.

Today they hauled off the skip, from which everything of value had been stolen. What remained was useless, broken

Vilhelm's Room

rubbish, because Vilhelm and Lise never got attached to things, and two people who leave each other for good every day for twenty years never acquire anything new or make any changes. I have even tossed all the photographs to better focus on the pictures on the walls of my heart. Only one have I kept: the photograph of Vilhelm and Lise at the top of Himmelbjerget. We are young and happy, and so obviously in love even the photographer must have been envious. For there is something about any fresh and new beginning that stokes a person's need to destroy the fragile construction, or at least to bring the bricks into disarray so it ends up crooked and unfinished and no longer catches anyone's eye. The strangest thing about great love is that it desires to be seen and exhibited, as if everything the happy couple does demands the whole world's attention. Later on, it is impossible to remember what you said to each other though it was terribly meaningful, and you hardly permitted yourself sleep because sleep meant not speaking. And before you knew it, silence became natural, and words only a kind of fever that occasionally overcame you. And later a menacing emptiness spread between the words, which you turned over in your mouth many times before setting free. The walls moved closer until there was not enough air in the room. You had to say something, anything, and even that became difficult, because the words had vanished into the bitter sadness of our souls.

All that is left (it was our last year in Birkerød) are words such as 'butcher', 'rain' or 'boy', and we rattle them off with dry, flat voices so nothing horrible will happen; to prevent a cruel and irreversible act. Was Vilhelm beautiful? His flawless skin had the colour of heavy cream with a dash of coffee. His cheekbones were high and seemed to pull the corner of his eyes towards his temples. His eyes were grey-brown with a dark ring around the iris, and beneath them, already then, the smoky shadows which betray a life of suffering and debauchery. I could not fathom how any woman could be happy without knowing him, just as years later I could not fathom how anyone could love him when I no longer did. But they could, or they did, and through their love for him (a demure, sweet flock of little hairdressers, shop assistants, office trainees and factory girls) my own was rekindled and drove away these poppy-flower girls, these faint sketches, these flimsy beginnings, from his enigmatic heart. My Vilhelm, mine!

To think that it would be Mille of all people who abducted him, this woman to whom I had become so attached I no longer knew who I missed most! Mille, who was neither young, nor beautiful or intelligent, but possessed a cold-heartedness that surpassed even ours when, exhausted by our peculiar passion, we lounged about amusing ourselves at the expense of the poppy-flower girls whose soft petals drifted limply away on the wind. Naturally, things could not continue in this manner, she wrote in her stupid letter. But what was all our suffering compared to the bliss of pleasure? Lise had felt an impotent rage when, six months earlier, she was informed that Vilhelm had become fat. Mille had force-fed him like a goose, stuffed and basted him and buried all his exquisite, dark thoughts under mountains of liver paté. With that, Lise's Vilhelm was dead and gone, and Mille filled her with disgust. Anger is always directed at the mistress, but once Lise annihilated the whole world, she reconciled with her too. And now, I will tell you my story, only because I must. And, of course, because no one else rightfully can . . .

2

Mrs Thomsen made a living by renting rooms to respectable young men from good families. At least, that was what she sought in her advertisements. I wouldn't rule out the possibility that such fresh-faced, downy fellows might, at the dawn of time, have resided somewhere in her enormous, filthy flat, but given that the mere sight of her is enough to make my blood run cold, I assume they got out as quickly as they could. Mrs Thomsen always suspected her lodgers of having a hand in every unsolved crime and likely did not sleep for fear of missing an incriminating piece of evidence during her tireless spying on their comings and goings. As for the rest, if they did not leave of their own accord, she eventually evicted them. And before she could even change the sheets, new ones would move in. At least that's what she told them, in her hoarse, wheezing voice that hobbled behind her thoughts like a stutter before steadying into a kind of monotonous drone when she got to the lurid descriptions of her former lodgers' unfathomable depravity and the impossible task – for a poor, sick old widow whose best days were behind her – of holding them accountable for their studies. Over time Mrs Thomsen's lodgers became less reputable and less young, and the only studying they dedicated themselves to was each morning counting up the bedbug bites acquired overnight.

The old woman was unmoved. She preempted any complaints by simply throwing them out. Often, the eviction took place with the help of the police, and she was fond of drawing the officers' attention to the recent spate of unsolved murders, which always occurred during the exact hours the suspicious lodgers had managed to evade her watchful eye. No doubt they would one day find her in bed with a slit throat, she usually added. I'm not disinclined to agree, for if souls such as hers even exist, God grants them a violent and sudden end. But it's no concern of mine whether Mrs Thomsen ever existed or not. She is a fragment of my dissolved consciousness, floating away on a swell of words, clinging to them and begging for help, just as I am begging the reader for help, yes, begging the reader even to love me, no matter how my face, blurry and ungraspable as if reflected in rippling water, may appear behind other faces far easier to hold on to.

We lived below Mrs Thomsen. Since she was rarely seen outside her flat, I had met her only on three or four occasions over the course of ten years. Each time, she stood very still, sizing me up as though she had sinister intentions and was sorry that the time had not yet come. Her eyes were bloodshot like those of an insomniac, and there was a purity to her ugliness that commanded a shuddering respect, but the look in her eyes was so cold and greedy that it scared me for days after our encounters. Her bedroom was directly above Vilhelm's room, and I could feel how her vile, slimy thoughts seeped through the ceiling and mingled inextricably with mine. I'm almost certain that she was lurking in the stairwell with a gristly, hairy ear pressed against the door the day Mille appeared in the living room and proclaimed: It's just awful! He's never coming back – after twenty-one years! And she flung out her arms and her face grew wet as if a button had been pushed to activate a hidden sprinkler system, and I lunged at her to stuff the words back in, along with her jumble of teeth which now came tumbling out, followed by the rest of Mille, skeleton included, until

Vilhelm's Room

all that remained was a little puddle. Mille's gentleness; her terrible lack of insight, her duplicity! And the boy, momentarily growing a few inches taller so he could glare through his eyes and use his father's voice: Get out, this instant! You've done enough harm.

Satisfied, the old woman must have hobbled back upstairs. She despised, without exception, all women who were younger and prettier than her, which just about amounted to the entire female half of humanity. She detested the myth of true love and on this fateful day she saw her doubt in its existence confirmed. – And yet, despite this, there was a faint shadow of such love present between the odious woman and the young man, discarded by both life and himself, upon whom she exerted such a morbid force of attraction that even her bad breath became integral to it.

Kurt, who did not really live, nonetheless had a life. When Mrs Thomsen entered his room in the morning, he always pretended to be asleep, but his heart pounded at the thought of what was about to happen. The air around him darkened, and as she limped towards him, chattering incessantly and rustling her ever-present newspapers, his body began to smoulder. He gently touched himself under the deceased Mr Thomsen's lumpy duvet which reeked so pungently of naphthalene that even the hungriest bedbug preferred starvation to coming anywhere near it. The landlady entertained him with outrageous tales of abominable thrill kills and ghastly fights to the death, which she had seemingly witnessed with the cold, analytic clarity of someone who intended to record her observations for a scientific study. Behind his twitching eyelids, Kurt saw infected guts tumbling out onto the operating table while inebriated doctors attempted in vain to stuff them back in. And with terror-stricken impatience, he awaited the climax when the patient would awaken mid-surgery and expel their last breath in a gush of blood and agonizing screams.

There were countless variations to this strange oratory performance, which Mrs Thomsen drew out as long as possible, punctuating it with sentimental tabloid tales of beautiful young women bravely facing their impending death by cancer, or an unfortunate family whose child's brutally maimed body had been found in a nearby rubbish bin the same night one of her lodgers had made himself scarce. But the woman never missed her mark. When her victim became short of breath, and his hands beneath the duvet honed in on a single burning point, she let her shabby blue bathrobe fall to the floor and threw herself over him with a passion only greater for its mingling with contempt. And finally he opened his bewildered doll's eyes, which brimmed with a kind of shuddering admiration for the immensity of force in so haggard a body. Afterwards, he promptly fell asleep and because he possessed a genuine lack of interest in other people, he never thought about the life his peculiar lover led when she was out of sight. Nor did he care, just as he never wondered why this victim of hundreds of failed surgeries still had not succumbed to any of them. The only explanation he could think of was that she, like the rest of the world, was a figment of his imagination. It was not something he dwelled on, for he had never felt compelled to analyse his life. Great things were once expected of Kurt, and he had indeed embarked upon a string of unfinishable studies before people had ceased to expect anything of him at all. But Mrs Thomsen, who never allowed anything of value to go to waste, and who, in addition, ascribed to others the same nasty qualities she herself possessed, had long been annoyed that this healthy, usable body should laze about in bed under her roof. One also cannot rule out the possibility that his happiness was a matter close to her heart, especially if it might lead to the unhappiness

Vilhelm's Room

of others. Besides murder and other macabre news, she meticulously pored over the classifieds each morning. So great was her eagerness to read the newspaper before anyone else that she often waited by the door, ready to catch it from the mail slot before it hit the floor.

This Sunday morning, Kurt was half-asleep in bed as usual while the knowledge of what would soon transpire unfurled deep within him like a fruit that had ripened overnight and was now waiting to be picked. But the blessed, horrifying, highly anticipated moment never arrived because, in her excitement, the old woman burst into the room without having taken the time to slap the customary greasy wig onto her bald head. (She had lost her hair during one of her failed surgeries, and the legal dispute with the doctor in question had yet to be settled.) Kurt stared at her aghast, convinced that the house was on fire, or that a homicidal knife-wielding lodger was at her heels. Then he spotted the newspaper in her trembling hands and suddenly felt very tired and very defenceless. The soft throbbing beneath his fingertips ebbed out, and he scrunched his narrow nostrils in displeasure when she sat down on the edge of his bed and jabbed a dry, stubby nail at a red-framed advert already conspicuous due to its length.

'It's her,' she hissed into his ear. 'Without a doubt. Read it! This is the chance of a lifetime.'

'Who?' Kurt recoiled towards the wall as if hoping it would swallow his frail body (which the landlady only fed meagrely and irregularly), letting him slip in between two layers of wallpaper and consuming him whole in its acrid dampness.

'The woman downstairs – Lise Mundus – the one with the love poems – I've told you often enough how they carry on. I knew it the moment I saw her and the boy return from their summer holiday alone. This last bint must've got the better of her and run off with him, the husband. You can always recognize a ruined woman – I certainly can: she couldn't have looked more naked had she not a stitch of clothing on. A month ago she was picked up and carted off in an ambulance, and not for the first time. Though the husband is none too handsome, it must be hell to have a lunatic for a wife. She's never deigned to greet me, but she's not above advertising for a new husband! At least I've never stooped to such lows.'

This entire tirade was delivered with such breathless fury, as if the old hag feared she wouldn't get it all out before her voice started to unspool. Kurt felt that if, in that moment, he'd had a knife and just a little more anger and energy at his disposal, he could have slit her throat in cold blood. Life was one long flight from one hiding place to another. From one dream to another, and in between the dreams, there was hunger and cold and fear –

He closed his eyes and sank deeper under the naphthalene duvet. Then, politely, he said:

'Mrs Thomsen, if you insist I read the advert, I kindly ask that you make yourself presentable in the meantime.'

He had never addressed the woman by her first name, in fact he did not know what it was.

Mrs Thomsen, who prided herself on etiquette, obediently retreated with a slurping sound as though sucking down an oyster. Kurt half-heartedly read the advertisement, trying to recall what he had heard about this woman. But it bled together with other stories of a similar nature: foul, seething tales from the gutter of humanity, the only world the old woman knew – perversions made all the more monstrous by being merely hinted at. Yawning, he let his eyes skim across the advert, summoning a stale ability to register only the most relevant details: 'Recently escaped a long, unhappy marriage – aged 51, but youthful in spirit – wonderful son, aged 15 – household literary name – summerhouse – large flat in the city centre – temporarily incapacitated by a nervous breakdown – prefers a motorist.' Kurt let the paper drop to the filthy floor and felt a sudden urge to see the sky. For almost twenty years he had lived in places where only small sections of it were visible between rooftops and walls. He shook his head and pushed the yearning back down into the sediment to which the past was relegated. He did not indulge in nostalgia, and when you never touch memories, they fade and disappear. The woman's age disturbed him, like the sight of childhood friends transformed by time into caricatures of the playmates you once knew. Kurt the Inadequate was scared of the terrible claim she would have on him. But Kurt the Good was slightly moved by the humble wish of 'prefers a motorist', yet not enough to distract from the opportunity it presented to evade his landlady's ruthless matchmaking. Red dots of exhaustion flickered behind his eyelids, because now it was over, the dream was over, and an infinite number of unforeseeable actions would become necessary. Throughout Kurt's life, just as he had grown accustomed to something, it would invariably have to change. And in this regard, his life was not so unlike other people's. There will always be a warm bed that needs filling after a death, and someone who will erase the sheets' comforting, intimate creases that formed overnight. There will always be a Mrs Thomsen to tell you it must end, and a Kurt the Good or Kurt the Terrible who must face up to it.

When the landlady, who by her own estimation was missing over half of her vital organs while the rest were in a critical condition, returned to her mystifying cave of pleasure, the sight was enough to extinguish any hopes of eluding change. Not only had she put on her wispy grey wig, but also something blue and floppy, reminiscent of a dress, which – whatever her intentions may have been – destroyed their bizarre morning ritual for good.

'You're right,' Kurt said, very gently. 'This is my chance.'

And someone or something woke up deep down in Vilhelm's abandoned room. A beam of cold sunlight whirled up the dust around the unmade bed, and there was a slight creaking from Hørup's collected works, which Vilhelm had stolen from the foreign minister when they were students once upon a time and neither of them dreamed of reaching the pinnacles of power upon which they now found themselves. The heavy drapes emitted a dank smell like cheap perfume infused with sweat. Perhaps the ceiling's stucco cherubs even wrinkled their noses at the stench of urine from the toppled floor vase Vilhelm would use when, in his drunkenness and despair, he couldn't bring himself to leave the room. Perhaps at this moment, one of the poppy-flower girls disentangled herself from some embrace, stirred by the memory of something incredible that once happened to her, something you must forget if you wish to go on living. And it isn't unthinkable that a whisper of all this passed through the terrifying landlady's heart when she, with a smile that exposed her milky-blue dentures, handed Kurt the Evader a pen and paper so he could respond to the advert.

What is certain, however, is that she was unaware that with this act she all but signed the death sentence of the only kind of love she had ever known.

3

Lise, who was no longer present within herself, awoke in the pale, blue vigil of night to find Greta sitting up straight in bed as if in a sarcophagus, staring at her with dry, burning eyes:

'I'm afraid of going mad.'

'Don't be,' Lise assured her, 'it's just your nerves.'

Seized by good spirits and a sense of well-being, she crawled under Greta's skin and with a capable hand forced the protruding thought back down into her crystalline depths. Soft and yielding, Greta's strong, beautiful body sank back onto the pillows, and she said in her usual mail-order bride voice:

'Turn on the lights, Lise. Let's have a smoke.'

This was her way of helping Lise avoid being present, and naturally she was unaware of doing so. Weeks of living together had simply taught her. She never gave Lise any choice to make. She decided for her, ordered her around and directed her every move. At this moment, she decided that Lise should not sleep but smoke. They lay propped up on their elbows beneath the reading lights and spoke in hushed voices, and it didn't bother them in the slightest that someone outside the room was screaming. It was just a newcomer who had not yet understood how things were done. The code of conduct forbade both smoking in bed and turning on lights at night, but no one was particularly concerned when those rules were broken. Meanwhile, if you showed signs of abnormal behaviour for extended periods of time, you'd be promptly kicked out of the locked ward for madwomen. And I'm sure most would agree that screaming at the top of your lungs in the middle of the night, running down the long corridors stark naked or, worst of all, smashing the flowerpots with which the kitchen lady and true leader of the ward, Mrs Vodskov, decorated the narrow windowsills, is not normal. For such audacity, even in one's first days, there was no excuse, and it no longer occurred to the weary head doctor to defend the transgressor during his hurried weekly visits. The few times he had tried, Mrs Vodskov had still made life here such hell for the culprit that it was worse than the hell outside, which you, my love, will know is no small feat. Of course, to the fools who still believe the world is governed by reason, it may seem as though they discharged the sick and kept the healthy, but Lise and Greta had placed the entirety of their fragile sense of safety in this muted, rule-governed madness where it was their most ardent wish to remain.

'The head doctor is coming tomorrow,' said Greta, 'may the Devil take him.'

'It'll be fine. I've taken two kitchen shifts, and you did gardening.'

To be entrusted with the nursery was a post coveted by all, unless they were keen to be discharged, which very few were.

'And tomorrow Kurt the Third is coming,' Lise laughed.

'You should say yes to this one,' Greta decided gravely. 'You can't keep rejecting them.'

'The last one looked like he'd been soaking in brine for six months.'

At the thought of him Greta couldn't help but laugh too. He was a short, fat, bald bank teller who wanted Lise's summerhouse sold, the money placed in bonds and her beloved son shipped off to boarding school. Like Man No. 1, he treated her to coffee and cheese sandwiches down at Café Skovly, then proceeded in a fatherly manner to assure Lise that she needn't trouble her little head with the business of money. He'd take care of it while she was here, recovering. His jaw dropped when he heard that Lise had left all her pesky finances to the social worker and didn't have anything to trouble her little head with except the management of her weekly hundred-kroner allowance.

The advertisement was Greta's doing. When one has been so unfortunate as to lose a husband, one must naturally find a new one and make certain demands of him without concealing one's own assets. Lise had obediently listed hers and only helped Greta with the spelling of the difficult word *literary*. The long, revelatory advert was, of course, merely a pretext to get Kurt the Disintegrated to seep down through the ceiling to Vilhelm's room, just as the negotiators and destroyers were pretexts, entirely insignificant in and of themselves. You and I too are pretexts for fateful interactions between people we don't know and will never meet. Only God sees the big picture, and he has no choice but to give in to all manner of amusing or cruel whims so as not to die of boredom up there in his high heavens.

Greta stubbed out her cigarette and cast a disapproving glance at van Gogh with the severed ear (or rather, without it) on the wall.

'He was the only one,' she mused, 'who didn't write anything about walks in nature.'

And here we will leave Lise and Greta for a moment – for they are doing well and have no need of us. While they babble cheerfully about marital candidates' manic obsession with rambling about in nature, we will even let the night outside come to a standstill; let it, for once, fall asleep, and in time it will be morning. Elsewhere lies Mille, staring with her dull raisin-eyes at my poor Vilhelm, in whom she has not yet managed to smother the memory of our brutal, merciless, rageful, tender life. But she is patient. It took her two years to move him from my bed to hers, and now there is no rush. He's sick and terrified and helpless, but she will get him back on his feet because, unlike the poppy-flower girls, she believes the thing she calls love can make miracles happen. She has scrubbed his back (my Vilhelm who only bathed on Three Kings' Day), dressed him in clean pyjamas and coaxed a bowl of soup into him. It's all quite sensible and quite ludicrous, and suddenly Mille's whole body quivers like a bony little bird. It is a purely physical exhaustion. She has been working like a horse to rescue this rare, precious person from a relationship that was killing him. For months she has watched him gorge himself on whisky and sleeping pills, which she has had delivered since she won't leave his side for a second. She has, without interrupting, listened to all his hateful, bitter accusations against the detestable woman Mille now feels she has never known, even though she once scrubbed her back too. She also scrubbed our homeless, pensive boy's back, until his dear face cracked open so she could stuff vitamin supplements and nutritious foods into his laughing mouth.

From time to time, she has overheard sweet, nighttime words intended for another and tolerated being called someone else's name in their brief, desperate unions that left no room for her own pleasure. And now the wicked Mille is tired. Her wickedness lies in her inability to see unhappy people without doing her utmost to make them happy. And the unhappy are drawn to her like the crippled and ailing to a holy spring. They pop up around her like poisonous mushrooms, more beautiful than dangerous if left to grow in peace. But Mille can't leave dark, impenetrable souls in peace. She must free the trees from the rot, even though it sustains them. Her tirelessness is formidable and only fails her at the most extreme point of exhaustion. For a second, at the sight of Vilhelm's pallid face beaded with sweat, the thin worm of doubt sneaks into her heart.

Then, while the night holds its breath at my command, we let her drift off too. The wicked, guileless Mille, whose true strength lies in her lack of wits, stretches her hardy, harmonious milkmaid body with its warm, soft nipples. She closes her heavy eyelids, tinged blue by the dark pupils beneath them. It's impossible for me not to like Mille a little bit, but no more so than I am fond of the repulsive Mrs Thomsen, of Kurt, of Greta and of Lise the Absent, for I exist in all of them. I watch over them while the night sleeps.

But now it's time to wake Kurt if he is to catch the train to Roskilde, dressed in a dead man's suit which Mrs Thomsen is already retrieving with her mangled hands from a secret hiding place.

4

They approached the café from either side, these two people who had come to be each other's last remaining chance. The previous night's laughter flittered away in Lise's wake, and despite the stiff oilskin hat Greta had fastened under her chin with a bow, the cold rain hit her face like hard, sharp fingernails, piercing the coat of tan make-up Greta had slathered on it to soften the twenty-year age difference. A few newly washed strands of hair tore themselves loose from the tea-lady updo Greta had spent hours constructing in front of the bathroom mirror, aided by the ward nurse, who knew her fair share about aberrations of the mind but was utterly ignorant of how a woman ought to look on the occasion of such an odd rendezvous. Like a partridge dragging its broken wing, Lise plodded along the wet gravel path, her movements awkward and jerky, her mascaraed, grey eyes fixed on the café's dripping thatched roof. The fear of Greta being discharged in her absence – Lise was the only one who had been permitted to leave the ward before the head doctor's arrival – outweighed all other fears in the world, and it drove away any thought of the young man waiting for her, just as the fear of ever having to see Mrs Thomsen again prevented Kurt the Persecuted from forming any impression of Lise when she sat down across from him with a smile on her painted lips not unlike that of a child about to cry.

'I've been looking forward to seeing you,' said Lise stoutly, seeing only a wet rag doll about to come undone at the seams.

Vilhelm's Room

'The pleasure is all mine,' Kurt lied in the well-mannered voice he had been taught by those who once had expected great things of him, though their lessons had proved a waste of time. With his young, pale face poking out from Mr Thomsen's much too big collar, he resembled a circus clown whose tragic expression only enhances the comedic effect. The waitress, who had long been curiously eyeing the peculiar guest, could not repress a delighted snort when she realized he was one of Lise's suitors. Kurt furrowed his brow as she approached, for he couldn't stand eliciting any sort of laughter from those around him.

'A coffee and cheese sandwich, as usual?'

'Yes, please,' Lise said without turning her head. Nervously she smoothed the tablecloth with a slender, cold hand, her nails embellished with Greta's pink mother-of-pearl polish. Would Greta remember what she had said? 'If they call you in, just tell them you're still having compulsive thoughts.'

'Shall I help you with your coat?'

Kurt made a half-hearted attempt to stand up, but Lise quickly beat him to it, taking off her coat and hanging it on the hook on the wall along with her hat. When she sat back down, lovingly swaddled in Greta's tea dress, both of them were seized by an urge to get to the point.

'How funny,' said Lise, 'that you live right above me.'

'Yes, but as I wrote in my letter, I can't stay there any more. Mrs Thomsen has rather put me in a bind.'

'You can move into my husband's room,' Lise promptly offered.

'But what if he comes back?'

'He won't.'

'And your son?'

'He won't mind.'

Their clipped, businesslike exchange brutally tore away the veil that separated Lise from the gruesome reality. She scrambled to grasp it again, pulling the collar of her dress tightly round her neck as though she suspected the man might rip off her clothes and rape her right then and there. She stared out at the rain while a few dulcet lines rose from her mind and spilled over her lips like lush blossoms:

> *Tears fall in my heart*
> *As rain falls on the town;*
> *What is this torpor*
> *Pervading my heart?*

Kurt wasn't listening. With a poor man's necessary short-sightedness, he was preoccupied with calculating how the remainder of Mrs Thomsen's paltry investment could cover both the bill and a taxi to the station. At least he had already bought his return ticket. The possibility of making the long journey on foot was just as unthinkable to him as allowing a woman to pay the bill in public.

'Verlaine,' Lise stated quite needlessly and tried to remember the parts of Kurt's letter that had stood out because Greta found them so appealing. Something about a law degree cut short, which sadly had not left him much spare time to dedicate to literature, despite it being one of his favourite subjects in school. Something about finding himself in a sticky situation – prospects of some sort – lonely, looking for love. Now Lise, whose unhappiness made her just as short-sighted as poverty made Kurt, wanted only to bring the ordeal to an end and get back home to deliver a satisfactory report to Greta, who is impatiently waiting for her in the room bathed in the orange light that filters through the always-drawn curtains. Suddenly she is once again so overwhelmed by the fear that Greta has been discharged while she has been sitting here, wasting time. So much so, in fact, that she feels compelled to assuage it at once.

'I just need to make a call,' she says, placing three ten-kroner notes on the table. 'In the meantime, you can pay the bill.' She's aware of his embarrassment, and this is an easy, tactful way of helping him overcome it.

'Greta,' she says breathlessly, 'has the head doctor been by?'

'No, don't worry, he has the flu. How are things with you?'

'Just splendid,' Lise rejoices, 'he's perfectly nice. And he complimented your dress.'

'Did he really? So I was right about his letter. Don't forget to give him the key to the flat.'

'Yes, but I should give him some money, too. I don't think he has a cent to his name.'

'Give him whatever you've got on you,' Greta orders, 'and you can send him a cheque tomorrow. And ask him whether he can cook. You said Mrs Andersen isn't very good at that.'

'I'll remember,' Lise promises, wrapped not only in Greta's dress but also her unconditional trust in young people with diplomas and impeccable diction.

With flushed cheeks she hurries back to the table, no longer resembling a maimed bird but something more akin to what Kurt had fearfully imagined, namely a woman of import. Now he's too tired to imagine anything at all, apart from a deep sleep in a soft bed under the duvet of a man he never knew.

He accepts the keys with a polite, distant smile and listens with his last dregs of attention to Lise's assurances that a cheque will follow tomorrow. He answers affirmatively to the question of cooking, and despite the relief of having found a way out of his predicament, like a rat spotting light at the end of a narrow sewage pipe, his pride is wounded by the undue haste with which Lise leaves him. He sits for a moment, watching the plump waitress with her glassy, expressionless doll's eyes. For some reason she's no longer laughing. Snatches of sentimental pop songs flutter through her, sweet and inconsequential, edged with a melancholy that prompts this otherwise hard-boiled soul quite uncharacteristically to place a beer in front of the poor young man, who is caught in Lise's web with no hope of escape. Kurt the Polite drinks it and, perhaps as a kind of thanks, says:

'I'm perfectly familiar with Verlaine.'

Then he tucks his head into Mr Thomsen's big white collar and falls asleep in the backseat of the taxi, while Lise the Absent dashes through the rain as if fleeing a house on fire. Her long, drenched hair hangs pitifully over her bony shoulders, and she is near fainting when she finally collapses in Greta's loving arms, gleefully telling her whatever she wants to hear. Greta has a husband with rough hands and a face of stone that never cracks. He drops his wife off here when she starts saying strange things and picks her up again when she stops. They have a grown daughter who has inherited his stone face and the duties that come with it. They never let down Greta the way Vilhelm let down Lise, and yet Greta's life is a nightmare. She falls into a stupor in a supermarket aisle, she drops stitches in the sensible knitwork of everyday life and forgets to have dinner ready at six o'clock when the stone faces come home from work. She stares transfixed at the babies in prams who study their adorable sausage-fingers with bright, inscrutable eyes – right until the angry mothers whisk them away. Eventually the police find her kneeling in an alleyway with a purring kitten pressed to her chest, and by that point Greta can neither remember her own name or address. And because it's impossible to wrest the soft, warm little creature from her grasp, she's allowed to keep it until the door here is locked behind her. Then the kitten is confiscated, and long, piercing wails cut through the air, as if a horrific beast had locked its jaws around her throat, and Greta does not realize they're coming from her. Only when the screams subside into childish, hiccupping sobs is she consumed by a fierce and silent terror of going mad; she who leads so sheltered a life and whose daily chores, so the stone faces assure her, are well within her capacity. Now she rinses off the remaining make-up from Lise's sodden face at the sink in the corner of the orange room.

'Was he handsome?' she asks Lise's wet neck.

'Very,' replies Lise, who has forgotten all about him. All she remembers is that his brown hair hung so far down his forehead it looked as if his eyebrows were holding it up, but she doesn't divulge such a strange observation to Greta.

5

With the blithe ingratitude that so perfectly befits spoiled children, the boy reaches out for the marmalade while Mrs Andersen, who always smells chastely of soap and ironing, painstakingly peels the shell off his egg. Between them sits Kurt, wearing Vilhelm's bathrobe, aching to go back to bed the minute the boy has gone off to school and Mrs Andersen starts airing out and tidying up. This fragile boy fills and defines Mrs Andersen's entire world, while her opinion of Kurt can be summed up in the few words she told her husband: He could be worse! By that she simply means that he doesn't steal the silverware, and that the boy, oddly enough, seems to like him. The boy's name is Tom, and with his long, straight, girly hair that is one shade lighter than his eyelashes, his delicate skin and slight build, he looks several years younger than he is. Only a very faint shadow above his thin upper lip heralds the distressing time to come when people will wonder whether the boy is growing a moustache or has simply forgotten to wash.

Satisfaction spreads across Mrs Andersen's moonlike face when she sees that the egg is neither too hard nor too soft. The boy rewards her with one of his fleeting smiles and slides what's left of the egg over to the finicky cat, who struts across the white tablecloth, sticking its rough tongue into the marmalade, the honey jar or the fresh butter. It's a brown Siamese and belongs to the boy, who, to Mrs Andersen's perpetual worry, constantly has little scratches on his arms and the backs of his hands after playing with it; the same boy who is otherwise so sensitive he still howls when he gets soap in his eyes, no matter how carefully Mrs Andersen washes his hair. She thinks of the time wicked Mille stole this privilege, which had been Mrs Andersen's ever since the boy was born as a wonderful substitute for that seed Mr Andersen never quite managed to sow at the right time and place. She had been so hurt by this sly act of treachery that she had ranted for nights on end to her good-natured husband about how dangerous this woman was – unlike her predecessors, who had, at least, kept their hands off the innocent boy. This will not end well, she had said, and the lady of the house is so trusting of others that she cannot imagine anyone would do her harm.

Inside Mrs Andersen, there were two sharply divided rooms. In one were the people she loved with no need to understand or criticize their baffling choices, and in the other was the rest of humanity, whom she held to the same strict moral standards as she did herself.

'Aren't you happy your mother is coming home today?' she asked.

'Yes,' said the boy with such a faraway look Mrs Andersen wasn't sure he had heard her. He hadn't told her about the dreadful things that had happened during her holiday, and she hadn't asked him. It must have pained him terribly when the entire press had found out about the advert without his poor mother being able to defend herself. There was, in Mrs Andersen's opinion, nothing wrong in the lady's advertising for a new husband, but there certainly was in the heartless journalists having discovered it.

The boy glanced at the newspaper that lay open between him and Kurt. A headline caught his eye: '10-Year-Old Boy Testifies Against Father.' He recalled a picture from his history book's chapter on the French Revolution: A little boy in a velvet suit with a ruffled white collar and his hands behind his back stands before a row of judges with smarmy grins. 'Where is your father?' read the caption. Despite the threat of gruesome torture, the boy kept saying he did not know. Just as Tom had said to Mrs Andersen, who had asked him only once. His father was at the mercy of Mille, exactly as Kurt had been at the mercy of the witch upstairs until he escaped to safety. When Tom was little and still lived with his mother in a dangerous yet thrilling world of his imagination, the beastly woman had once grabbed him in the stairwell as he was returning from school. He had screamed bloody murder, and his father had come rushing out, tearing him from her greedy claws. 'Keep your filthy hands off my son,' he had shouted, enveloping the boy in his warm, protective embrace. The boy had told Kurt about it, and Mrs Andersen would have been green with envy had she known that Tom had also confided in this dubious stranger of all people, this man unplaceable in either of her heart's two chambers, telling him and no one else about the triumphant day when he had single-handedly thrown Mille out, doing what needed to be done to protect his mother. It had all transpired in a daze. With his arms crossed like in 'The Prince with the Cold Heart' – the school play he had once starred in – he had shown her the door. 'Then the bitch ran off,' he told Kurt, 'and I dialled ooo. Mum only came to in the ambulance.' And when Kurt, who identified with the boy, which was the closest he could come to liking him, expressed his eloquent admiration for this heroic deed, Tom had modestly replied: 'I only did what my father would have done.'

In the dining room with its high ceilings and old-fashioned, shabby elegance hung a dry, warm, dusty smell. Vacantly, Kurt stared at a stain on the wall that looked like a long, brownish teardrop. It was the mark left by a plate of roast lamb Vilhelm had once hurled in one of his hysterical fits. The boy had told

Vilhelm's Room

Kurt about this incident and others like it as if they had taken place solely for his amusement. 'And Mum?' he said, with his distinct mix of childishness and maturity, 'She wept and screamed, of course, but in fact she couldn't live without it.'

He wasn't looking forward to his mother's return nearly as much as Mrs Andersen liked to believe. He doesn't love her any less than he always has, but his love is now tinged with worry. How will she survive without his father?

He reaches out his lanky, tan, down-covered arms, awkward and endearing like a baby goat, and then all three of them freeze mid-movement, as if posing for an invisible camera which catches a snapshot with a soft click that makes the door to Vilhelm's room swing wide open. A sharp, putrid smell like old water in a flower vase wafts along the skirting board, and a cruel, heartbreaking laugh makes the stained walls slope inwards while the lifeless eyes of the stucco cherubs remain fixed on the warm dent in Vilhelm's pillow. The destruction has already begun, and the negotiators know it.

'Judging by the advert,' one says, 'the husband won't be coming back.'

'No,' his wife agrees, 'not now that she has disgraced him.'

'The question is whether she can afford to keep the flat.'

'Isn't it illegal to take in lodgers?'

'Not according to the lease, otherwise we would have kicked out Mrs Thomsen and her lot long ago. No, what I'd like to know is how much does her writing bring in?'

That same question preoccupies Greta, who, as if for the last time, is washing Lise's hair in the bathroom. But she doesn't ask. No one here does, apart from the no-nonsense Mrs Vodskov, who is standing in the doorway with her hands on her hips like the handles of a fat-bellied pot. She has sent four children into the world, into good positions with decent wages, and she is not nearly as impressed with this fellow at Lise's house as Greta is. A textbook marriage fraudster, she tells her husband that evening. He works as a caretaker and, like her, has no patience for people over thirty with unfinished degrees and uncertain prospects. Mrs Vodskov doesn't usually trouble herself with concerns about the futures of patients once they're out of her sight. But it's different with Lise, who wrote a song for her youngest's confirmation, thereby securing herself both a lasting place in Mrs Vodskov's heart and a lifelong exemption from weekly kitchen duty.

'Mrs Mogensen,' she says (no one here ever uses Lise's real surname), 'how much do you have left over each month, after taxes and rent have been paid?'

Greta sends her an indignant look, and Lise, of whom only a soapy neck is visible over the edge of the sink, does not hear her. Fortunately. Tears pour from her eyes, which are covered by a washcloth meant to shield them from soap. They're brought on by the grief of separating from Greta, whose own tears are kept in check by the task of making Lise presentable to meet her young lover, whose daily life with the boy Greta finds fantastical and uncomplicated like an old-fashioned serial. Lise, meanwhile, doesn't seem interested, and she hardly reads the letters Kurt sends her. It's enough to know that something living has been installed in Vilhelm's room, and that this being appears to please her poor, abandoned little boy, who, in Lise's mind, hasn't aged past twelve. Just like Kim, the boy in her children's books. While she writes them, she calls her son by the character's name, for the brave, valiant Kim is Tom's hero. Hand in hand with his mother, he has often walked along the city's ramparts, picturing the dangerous savages in the Kim books. They sleep during the day and spend their nights pillaging, a switchblade tucked in the back pocket of their raggedy trousers. Silent as cats they creep through the winding streets, and in the morning the boy scarcely dares go to school for fear of finding an officer slumped outside the front door with a knife in his back. And yet, he's mildly disappointed when there isn't one. The gang leader wears red socks and tennis shoes and has black curls just like Kurt.

And Kim hates women the same way Kurt and the boy hate the old woman upstairs. Maybe the 'wonderful son, aged fifteen' was what confused Tom most about the baffling advert that has troubled him so. Childhood is releasing its hold on him, but he squeezes into it like a pair of too-small trousers that can no longer be buttoned, even when he sucks his belly in. No one is interested in a grown-up Tom. No one has any use for someone so unthinkable. He knows – unconsciously – that his mother stops loving her children once they grow up. Then she starts behaving as timidly as a child herself around them, and she's content to know that they are healthy and not too unhappy. Tom has two grown half-siblings who are so much older than him that they were never children at the same time. When his mother is in hospital (strange to think that she was once their mother too), they call him or drop by and ask if there's anything they can do. His sister, twelve years his senior, whom he's never seen much of, sent him to Roskilde shortly after his father's disappearance to persuade their mother to sell the summerhouse as quickly as possible, so that his father – or rather Mille, towards whom all anger was directed – could not claim half of it.

And when it comes to practical advice of this kind, Lise follows it, even though she's unable to gauge the consequences. She signed over power of attorney to her distant daughter, who knew about such things, authorizing her to sell the house. To Lise, receiving a sizable sum and two mortgage deeds which could, in a pinch, be sold for cash felt like being awarded a grant. Depositing the money into her bank account gave her an incredible sense of security, but when, for the first time in her life, her balance exceeded one hundred thousand kroner, she received a tax bill for sixty-six thousand. The solicitor who had overseen the sale of the house advised her to pay the money and be grateful for what she had left. After that experience, she again pushed the world away, like an unreasonable child whose pestering would have to wait. Since those happy years in Birkerød, she hasn't known poverty, and she couldn't bear being both poor and unhappy at the same time. Not to mention the boy, who has never been refused anything on the grounds that it was too expensive. Now he blames himself for leaving the summerhouse early simply because he couldn't get a proper night's sleep; because his father's voice raged and screamed incessantly like a cursed wind blasting through his head, in one ear and out the other. And his mother screamed too, screamed and wept, begging him to at least spare the boy. And Tom's heart pounded so hard he couldn't take it and couldn't make it stop. So he rode his moped back to the city, rang up his friends, filled the flat with them, and forgot everything that frightened him until his heart felt like any other heart once again. Then he called his mother and asked whether his father was still there, because if he was, Tom would not go back. 'Just come,' said Lise, 'he's with Mille.' She spoke calmly, as if his father had gone to hospital, somewhere he was both cared for and rendered harmless.

Tom rode back to the summerhouse, and his mother was happy, Kirsten the holiday maid was happy, and they played cards and solved crossword puzzles, and that's when it began: no one mentioned Vilhelm's name, but everyone was thinking about him. We thought: Dear God, let him stay there as long as possible. Let it have passed by the time he returns. Let him enjoy Mille's 'magnificent build' (as though she were manufactured at Burmeister, Tom and I joked). Let him relish Mille's vitality, let him admire how 'she's never idle'. (She possesses an impressive knack for neverending, pseudo-sensible undertakings that never lead to any apparent results.) Give poor, brave Mille who only wants the best for all of us the strength to endure this cocktail of whisky and sleeping pills until he again becomes our great father, until he says: my little wife, and: my only son, my pride and joy. And above all: Let him not show up at the publisher's luncheon. He will ruin everything, he will make us so terribly afraid. Tom's heart will again pound so hard he'll think he's dying. And I, Lise, will have to pretend for these amiable yet aloof guests that all this is completely normal. Inevitably, these ridiculous scenes always play out when we have company, who are probably relieved that things are not this way in their homes, though, really, things are simply different there, and not one bit better.

But it made no difference that no one mentioned his name, because he arrived shortly after the guests, after all the eager preparations during which Lise had felt so happy and so hopeful that every step became more like a dream. She poured aquavit into their glasses and said something that made the publisher laugh. Everyone laughed, and this, the boy thought, is how things could always be if only his father hadn't changed so horribly, if only Mille would lie down flat like a doormat that scrapes the dirt off one's shoes before one treads on the parquet floors. Dear God – and suddenly, there he was, this father standing in the doorway at the most dangerous stage of his inebriation, foam at the corners of his mouth and sheer madness in his bloodshot eyes. 'Why, how quaint,' he muttered, rubbing his dry hands together so it sounded like sandpaper, and there was no other sound in the world, and the boy watched as his father staggered towards the table, but then, with a screech like a frightened bird, he bolted past him and leapt onto his moped, its saddle burning through his trousers because it had been parked in the sun all day. Not until he was many kilometres away did his heart calm, and he hadn't seen his father since, and his mother never told him what had happened after his escape that day. He was no 'wonderful boy';

he was a selfish idiot who had loved the feeling of Mille's long, cool fingers sliding through his hair when she washed it!

'It would never have happened if the boy hadn't gone home,' says Lise, while Greta vigorously rubs her hair with the towel, unaware that she will never see her friend again. With her talent for heartfelt hypocrisy, Lise has promised to write and visit, carefully noting down the address of the stone faces on a scrap of paper that promptly drifted from her hands and mind like the withered petals of the darling poppy-flower girls along the skirting board in Vilhelm's room. She doesn't even remember what Greta looks like any more. If, in a few hours, her body were brought to the morgue, Lise wouldn't be able to identify her.

Her grief disappeared down the drain, along with the water and tears.

'He needs to start living his own life soon,' Greta murmurs. 'He's almost all grown up.'

But Lise has regained her dangerous ability to hear only what she wants to hear. She exists in neither the present nor the future. The last thing she remembers of her real life is the day which was to be its conclusion – at least, for now. There is something about that day she has yet to make sense of. Again and again, her thoughts have brushed across all that transpired, light as a cat's paws on piano keys, so softly they make no sound. Mille couldn't know that Lise had taken those pills to escape the mounting, intolerable fear that Vilhelm might never come back to her. Strangely, it helps Mille's defence that even in her wildest dreams, she never imagined Lise would collapse in her arms, unconscious. The last human voice Lise heard was the boy's: proud, heartbreaking and lonely. Her final bewildered thought as she looked up at Mille's jiggling cheeks and chin: She isn't even pretty!

6

(Open letter to my Vilhelm)

My dearest, it is difficult to be so utterly alone and see no one but the paper shufflers with their clammy fish skin that grazes mine every so often when they hand me something to sign, try as I might to avoid it. It is difficult never again to sleep with my face in the warm, damp crook of your armpit and the comforting sound of your stiff, stubby eyelashes scratching the pillow. Meanwhile, you miss peculiarities of mine of which I am wholly unaware, for no two people ever experience the same thing at the same time. Perhaps we all exist in small, sealed-off rooms with no connection to each other, and we can endure it only because we are not aware of it. Growing older means calmly turning all one's experiences over in the light, examining even the most painful without fear. At last, one knows they will not recur. There is no time for it, no chance of it, and the furious passion which once drove us beyond all norms and conventions, all the limits imposed upon our urges by people who lived before we were born, this passion has now faded and blurred: a proud yet fragile memory of two people who can no longer tolerate the touch of others. I don't know where you live now, only that it is a place furnished in someone else's taste, or perhaps that of some third person. For you have never been one to create a home, and like me, you have inherited nothing. We often spoke of how happy we were that summer in Hornbæk, when our boy was one and had just learned to walk. But by then, unhappiness had already been set underway, invisibly like cells growing inside the body. No camera registers as ruthlessly as the young lover's eye once the initial wave of blindness has subsided. The heart suspects nothing yet, but a certain image can now never be erased. It may take years before it resurfaces, or it may take days.

We were lying on the beach up in Hornbæk, only a few minutes' walk from our rented house. We had fallen asleep in the blazing sun, and our shoulders had turned bright red. It was late in the afternoon. We had gone swimming several times, and I'd had enough. I felt a bit cold after my nap. There were many people around us, and we observed them as if through the bars of a cage. Without realizing, we had been doing so for the past three years. We stood outside the cage, free to approach them if we liked, but they could not reach us. Since I didn't want to join, you went swimming alone while I sat with my hand shading my eyes, watching as you waded carefully through the shallow water so as not to cut your bare feet on a rock or something sharp. Then, all at once, it struck me: He's no longer young! It was in the way you carried yourself and the hesitancy of your movements, a faint whisper of decay, almost imperceptible, but it was there, I had seen it, and from now on it would only worsen, and there was something unbearably sad about it, and I had to blink up at the sun to keep the tears from spilling over.

In that moment, tenderness made its way into my desire for the first time, and when that happens, one loves more intensely but far less sensually. You were thirty-five; I was two years older. We had both lived long lives before we met. I had three children by three different men. You had a daughter you never saw. You were already orphaned while my parents were still alive. Yet nothing in our shared life bore any resemblance to our prior, separate ones. All that had been stuffed behind the

Vilhelm's Room

bars we liked to stare through, but we had started using other people, Vilhelm, without for a second considering they had a life of their own, and that we were intruding on this life, perhaps even altering its course. I think it is very dangerous to live out one's most secret dreams. Hearing the details of your affairs with other women was painful, but it also aroused me, which is why I found our marriage a little boring when you were faithful for long periods of time. At that point, I had only been unfaithful once, half by accident, entirely absurd: a swift ambush by the old artist in the bedroom after he had explained to my mother and father, whom I had invited to lunch that day, that the light in there was much better than in the dining room. When I told you about it (for sinister reasons I only later understood), you stewed in your unreasonable jealousy, then insisted I recount every minute detail over and over again, and the old lecher would have been both flattered and mystified had he heard my lies and juicy exaggerations about the little sparrow-affair. The story quickly grew stale, but it had become clear: we were no longer enough for each other. I wonder whether you also watched me when I believed myself unobserved. And perhaps you thought: It shows that she has given birth three times. But then you read my poems. A selection of them would be published in the autumn, and some were inspired by my love for you. It's incredible how much that means to a man, even one as clever as you. They weren't even the best poems in the collection. By then, your admiration had already begun to yellow and fray with malice and envy. When I showed you the poem I was most pleased with, to my disappointment, you merely shrugged and said, 'You couldn't have written that had I not opened your eyes to the poetry of Rilke.' Of course, you were right, and since then I have never liked his work.

On that fine, clear day, I didn't even know where you worked exactly, let alone what your work entailed. You were always complaining that you were given no opportunities, no challenges. In the evenings, you'd pace restlessly across the living room, burdened with self-doubt, slapping your forehead with the flat of your hand and saying, 'How did I become such a failure?' I didn't understand how a head of department could be considered a failure, and above all, I didn't understand why being married to me wasn't proof enough of your worth! But I never said as much. The children and I didn't dare interrupt you when you were in one of your moods. Frantically, you asked me whether you should join the party, and since I didn't know which party you were referring to, I advised against it. That summer, in my newfound tenderness for you, there was a hint of triumph, as though I had won some strange victory over you. When one is no longer in love with a man, one cannot believe anyone else could be either, and so one glides, liberated, into a sense of security both fragile and false, like skating on thawing ice. Is Mille now revelling in that same security, I wonder? She doesn't drink, has never been addicted to pills as I was, and is undoubtedly as faithful to you as a gas meter or a clothes wringer. When she slices cucumbers, she rubs the last slice on her face because it's meant to be good for the skin, though hers is clear and unblemished to begin with. Sometimes the seeds stick to her black eyelashes, and you pluck them away with a laugh. For a while, you really were in love with her. Everything about her is different to me. She doesn't even smoke. She's so healthy it's nauseating. My dear, dear Vilhelm, there is one thing you will never persuade her to do: sleep with another man to satisfy you! Helene obliged and that allowed her to hold onto you for five years, but people can't live like that forever. When you moved back in with me after six months with her, you looked like an old injured tomcat who only returns home to die. My schoolmate Alice, who spotted me one day in Birkerød and watched us walk home from the station, completely

Vilhelm's Room

enamoured with each other, once told me: That's not a man one can grow old with! Her husband, on the other hand, looked as if she had chosen him solely with that in mind, but she was right all the same. Each of us must grow old alone. And only I, at least for a while yet, have the courage to do so.

Nothing in this room betrays its inhabitant. Behind me, the cat sleeps atop my duvet. It, too, is growing old. Occasionally a tremor ripples across its delicate shoulder blades, which have become so sharp of late. It hisses weakly at my touch, and one morning I will find its body limp and cold, a damp patch beneath it. Its big blue eyes are already hazy, foretelling an imminent, peaceful death. Often it stares at me with an expression of bewildered hostility, as though I could have prevented this strangeness from taking root inside it. It is the same look the old widower gave me behind the backs of the incessantly chattering negotiators when we stepped in here, the room where his wife had peacefully passed away. After fifty years of happy marriage, he insisted – vehemently, as if expecting me to contradict him. Yet he has presumably only known the tiniest sliver of her. Behind the red, tasselled velvet drapes hangs a white muslin blind, smelling about as fresh as the bolts of fabric in the old haberdashery shops that are steadily disappearing. The blind never really keeps the darkness out, the old man admitted apologetically, but one must respect a dying woman's last wish. We must have passed the two of them countless times without noticing them, because we only saw the parts of the world we had use for, just as we only ever saw in each other what we needed. Mille saw something in you that she needed, and when I think of her now, an angry, abandoned little animal stirs within me, baring its claws. For a long time, we felt the same for her as we did for her predecessors; a kind of affection built on the awareness of our power to destroy, a feeling made all the sweeter by being mixed with contempt. I still don't understand how this liver-pâté-baking health fanatic managed to push my hand away from the hot, pulsating core of your being while her mouth sought mine and clouded my senses with a breath as cool and pure as water from a mountain spring. Reality is unimaginative yet astonishing. What kind of terrifying game had she drawn us into? When did she begin to gain the upper hand? Perhaps none of it was planned; it simply happened.

It wasn't me who wrote those naïve, pleading letters – it was Greta, my fellow patient at St John's. I didn't even bother to read them; just signing them required enormous effort. Greta was livid with Mille for snatching you away from me and Tom. Greta always thought in such conventional terms, but that offers no security either. Nothing does. Mille's reply arrived three weeks later. Three wild weeks during which even the bed linens caused me physical pain, as if they were full of sharp needles piercing my skin day and night. I couldn't stand being inside my own body, so instead imagined I was nowhere, that this suffering shell encased a memoryless soul for whom it was a dull, bitter relief to analyse the effects of refined torture now that it no longer held the pleasure of being voluntary. I told Greta, who would have preferred to endure these torments in my place (you know how some humble, anonymous girls are), that Mille was fifteen years younger than me, divorced and childless. Mille's letter was simply insane, and Greta couldn't understand why it made me cackle like some croaky, vicious bird. I realized it was the first time I had heard myself laugh since that luncheon at the summerhouse before you showed up. I only remember the first and last sentence: 'It will please you to know that Vilhelm is much improved' (Vilhelm who?) and – 'otherwise, there is nothing new to report.'

It's odd that people don't fear each other more than they do, for they certainly have reason to. The chasm separating you from the person closest to you is reason enough, but perhaps most people aren't even aware of it. Still laughing, I opened the drawer of the nightstand and handed Greta the crazy advert I had hesitated to publish until that very moment. 'Just send it in,' I said, 'the worst has already happened.' My head felt lighter, as if an emptiness had swept through it; a mighty broom clearing away all complicated, despairing thoughts. The world edged closer, still wanting something of me, and I, afraid yet ready to fight, no longer wanted to push it away. The destruction had begun, and the negotiators woke in the middle of the night, not knowing why. The doctor stood in this room of death, checking the old lady's pulse. And on the train, the boy sat with his note from school. It was a permission slip that needed a parent's signature to excuse him from the school milk scheme, and he wasn't about to ask you for anything. All of a sudden, everything began to move, taking on direction with no clear end, driven by that peculiar force found within utter despair and its streak of cruelty, demanding either transformation or annihilation.

7

Despite much evidence to the contrary, Mrs Andersen had always upheld the illusion of serving a noble household. Essential to this concept – however much she had been forced to stretch its definition in recent years – was the indissolubility of marriage. When she returned from her summer holiday, spent at the same boarding house every year, and learned of what had happened, she locked the door to Vilhelm's room and did not set her sturdy foot in there again until Lise telephoned from the hospital and requested in that polite little voice of hers, so much like the boy's, that the room be prepared for Kurt's arrival. Mrs Andersen made do with emptying the foul-smelling vase, washing the floor and putting fresh sheets on the bed, which was still far more than what Mrs Thomsen's so-called lodgers were accustomed to. The poor lady of the house had been home for a month now. Christmas was approaching, and Mrs Andersen had only one sleeve left to finish on the jumper she was knitting for the boy.

'I think people are starting to forget about the advert,' she said, not looking up.

Her husband deemed a response unnecessary. Of late, such remarks bubbled out of his wife like water from a pot of potatoes left boiling on a stove one has forgotten to turn off. And he was too curious to turn it off by, for instance, switching on the television, or jokingly asking whether the coffee would brew itself. He sat in his rocking chair (a gift from the nobles on his sixtieth birthday) and smoked his pipe with the same look of shrewd naiveté with which he interrogated suspects at the station. He was a detective inspector, and his opinion of drunken editors-in-chief absconding from wife and child, or deranged female writers tarnishing their good name and reputation by publishing such blatantly transparent advertisements, he wisely kept to himself. Mrs Andersen let off a little more steam.

'Kurt is really quite cultured,' she said, vigorously clicking her knitting needles, which signalled to him that it was time to gently steer her thoughts elsewhere.

'In any case, it's good that the boy is so fond of him,' he said.

And then, as if prompted by an invisible director's cue, they both glanced towards the photograph of the Prince with the Cold Heart propped on the sideboard alongside a row of nieces and nephews, real children of flesh and blood possessing none of this delicate boy's fairy-tale beauty, or the expression of proud arrogance the role demanded – unless, of course, the boy had been chosen for the role precisely because of that look. Mrs Andersen had attended the performance and, like the rest of the audience, had been greatly amused by the way the prince had covered his mouth with his hand when he kissed the princess.

A dampened merriment spread through the glistening streets as the artificial lights anticipated the stars. The cold rain had given way to a fine cobweb of mist which blurred all sharp contours, much like the bowl-shaped sconces that softened the reflection of the naked Vera Lindblom, who tenderly cupped her small, tanned breasts in her hands. Vera loved her body and assumed that everyone else did too. If a man proved immune to its erotic allure, she figured he was either gay or impotent, and as for women, she always went to great lengths to soothe their understandable envy. In general, she held little regard for her own gender, apart from a certain solidarity with those employed in the same industry. But Lise Mundus was different. She emanated a special glow only made brighter by that magnificent advert, in which Vera discerned a sophisticated form of revenge against Vilhelm. Vera intended to strike a devastating blow to this man, Denmark's tabloid mogul, by interviewing Lise – an interview she, ahead of all bloodhounds, had finally managed to secure. With a coquettish flick of the arm, she tore herself from her captivating reflection and proclaimed:

'This is the greatest scoop of my life. Fetch my green pantsuit, will you?'

She was speaking to a man already fading into a shadowy outline, like the buildings in the fog outside. Vera preferred married lovers because they were easier to get rid of.

'Why do you hate Vilhelm?' asked the shadow, flipping through her wardrobe, which spanned an entire wall in the bedroom.

'Because he doesn't take his work seriously,' she replied, carefully selecting a smokey-blue eyeshadow from the multitude of pastel-coloured jars and compacts on the dressing table. But hatred, she thought, was too strong an emotion and just as much a hindrance to her career as love. Her nature was so akin to a man's that any semblance of routine or habit promptly stifled all desire. Still occupied with her make-up, she stated sweetly, without turning her head:

'I think you should go back to your wife and children. It won't do you any good to be with a girl who puts her work above all else in the world.'

The shadow began to move and the mirror fogged briefly, as if from someone's tears – that was all. Vera felt as if a velvety bat had been released from her mind, where it had been confined for far too long. Then the door slammed, and she let out a laugh, free of any cruelty. The whole city laughed along, producing a melodious din that drowned out a heart's soft lament. Everything was in motion, and now nothing could be stopped. Mrs Thomsen's raspy voice reached Mr Andersen's ear through the phone. It hissed about the latest heinous crime her former lodger Kurt Lorenzen had committed. Although the detective inspector was used to her unhinged reports, he did not, as was his habit, put down the receiver to attend to other matters until the old hag had finished talking. He knew full well that it was all manufactured lies, yet this Kurt had, in fact, come to play a role in the detective's life ever since he had wriggled his way downstairs like a regular silverfish, albeit one resistant to vacuuming. Could there be a grain of truth to the hag's abhorrent confessions? She spoke of a suitcase full of evidence, and Mr Andersen remembered that his wife had intended to retrieve Kurt's suitcase, which the 'poor old thing' upstairs apparently refused to surrender. Something was going on in that flat, and Andersen did not like it one bit. When the voice finally fell silent, he hung up the receiver and lit his pipe, deep in thought. He fancied himself as Maigret from Simenon's novels, which he devoured one after the next. What if he had stumbled upon a truly major case? Mrs Thomsen's talent for implying the most dreadful obscenities without accusing anyone outright roused in this phoney Maigret memories from his boyhood, which he usually never thought of.

Meanwhile, Tom lay in bed in his room listening to what his mother called canned music. It calmed him; silence was dangerous. He skimmed an issue of *Weekend Sex*, focusing mostly on the classifieds. Something about plimsolls and elasticated-waist trousers, with the crucial addition: intercourse unwanted. The homeless on the ramparts of Christianshavn no longer struck him as thrilling. They were just drunkards who slept in the local shelter once autumn set in, and he felt tricked into believing that becoming a grown-up would finally grant him access to the beguiling secrets he had previously had to eavesdrop at doors to uncover. He curled up with the cat and fell asleep to its purr.

Inside Vilhelm's room, Kurt was reading Vilhelm's diaries, spurred by a vague curiosity, as if he had boarded a train bound for an unknown destination. One of the last dated pages read: 'I hate her so deeply I fear the worst should I not manage to break free soon. Today, I spat in her face and tore off my shirt in a powerless rage. No reaction. She knows all too well that the aggressor loses the upper hand.'

8

Vera rummaged in her purse a bit longer than necessary to retrieve a notepad and pencil. Lise's appearance had shaken her a little. She looked thin and aged, sitting there on the sofa with her legs tucked under her. Vera had been expecting that, however. What caught her off guard was the aura of loneliness that enveloped this woman – unusual in its intensity yet entirely useless as an observation for the article. When she emerged from the depths of her purse, she had donned a warm, charming smile, as if it too had been retrieved among the purse's contents. Quick as a bird, her eyes flitted about the room: fashionable furnishings from Illums Bolighus, devoid of personal touches except for a cheap globe on the windowsill. It was cracked along the equator and reassembled crookedly, giving Vera an idea for her opening line: 'Lise Mundus is used to seeing her world split in two.'

'That advert was simply splendid,' she said.

Lise laughed, and a sudden sparkle lit up her eyes – the same one that, at a staff party several years ago, had made it apparent to everyone why Vilhelm, despite his persistent efforts, would never truly manage to extricate himself from her. It would have been what was best for the paper. At least, back then. When one is struggling with the near-impossible task of resurrecting a dying newspaper, one ought not to be saddled with a famous wife who has a penchant for killing herself at the most inopportune moments. But now Vera worked for a different paper, and Vilhelm was finally about to be publicly exposed.

'It was mad,' said Lise, suddenly looking like someone who had never smiled in her life. 'Can I offer you something to drink?'

'Maybe a glass of wine, if you have it?'

Lise disappeared into the shadows of the flat, and while she was gone, Vera was overcome by an unsettling sense that she was not alone. The sound of a stack of books toppling and a man coughing softly confirmed the feeling. The noises came from the other side of the closed double doors behind her. She sighed with relief and dismissed her initial impression of Lise. Apparently, the advertisement had yielded results. On her notepad, she jotted down: 'Lise Mundus has found a new man.' That would make for a good headline. From the long hallway that led to the kitchen, she heard Lise laughing and talking to someone; presumably her son. She was still laughing as she entered the room, balancing a tray in her hands and kicking the door shut with her heel. Her feet were clad in stockings, black ones. Her sleeveless dress was also black, cinched at the waist with a wide, shiny patent-leather belt, but something was missing – a piece of jewellery or a small scarf – to draw attention away from the loose skin under her chin. All the little feminine tricks one already adopted when approaching forty, like Vera herself, who, in addition to a soft angora jumper, wore oversized teardrop-shaped smoked topaz earrings that matched her skirt.

'Do you know,' said Lise as she curled up in her corner again, 'why all Aarhusians only take a half-hour lunch break?'

'No?'

'Any longer and they'd all need rehab!'

Vera laughed even though she had heard the joke before.

Lise filled the glasses to the brim, spilling clumsily like a nervous or unseasoned hostess. Her long, fair hair fell across her face. It was streaked with greys, but they were only visible directly under the lamplight. Her hair was freshly washed, but beyond that she seemed to care little about her appearance.

'Before I forget,' said Vera, tapping the ballpoint pen against her straight teeth. 'Would it suit for the photographer to come tomorrow at two o'clock?'

'Sure.'

To Vera's surprise, Lise downed the wine in a single gulp. Was she really an alcoholic? The wildest rumours circulated about her, but they were none of the readers' business. The purpose of this piece was to paint a sympathetic picture of a brave woman who, despite almost insurmountable loss, had kept her head high and was fully immersed in writing her next novel. A photograph of Lise beside the boy would be ideal, along with the coughing, book-toppling outcome of the advert. That would surely flush Vilhelm out of hiding. *Billed Bladet*'s bloodhound had sniffed out his new address in Frederiksberg, where, oddly enough, 'fashion model Miss Mille Bertelsen' also lived. Only a man, thought Vera disdainfully, could get his facts so wrong. The mistress was no fashion model. She was a divorced woman of about forty, childless, and with an inconsequential past. Vilhelm had met her when he was the editor of the weekly where she worked with abridged translations of penny dreadfuls. Nevertheless, the brief notice had alerted Vera to the fact that Vilhelm had yet again moved out. The last time this happened, word had also leaked to their inner circle, but that was before turning the private lives of famous people into tabloid fodder had become the norm. The average man on the street had no idea who Vilhelm was. However, he – and especially she – did know Lise: the gentlest, most girlish, most graceful and poetic writer, all these exaggerated superlatives whipped up by the press which corresponded so poorly to the advertisement's description that Vera decided to forego them – at least in part. Lise's tired eyes were fixed on an indeterminate point behind Vera's head, and Vera felt a twinge of anger, which served the story as little as her pity did. But she had to give it an outlet.

'You're very photogenic,' she said. 'Perhaps you should wear a dress with long sleeves, though. Do you still have the one from the staff party?'

Lise didn't catch this hint that she should cover her thin arms and pointy, dry elbows.

'What fun I had at that party, once he finally left,' she mused dreamily.

'Then you must be absolutely ecstatic now, right?'

'He was gone for eight days. When you were sent to fetch him, you said to him, "It's not for Lise's sake, it's for the paper's." He told me everything back then, you know. In any case, it worked. When I went to collect him the next day, he followed me home. Ever since, we've called it "the Encyclopaedia Crisis"!' She gestured as if cracking a whip and finally met Vera's eyes with a look of mischievous satisfaction that upended all of Vera's preconceptions. *Enigmatic*, she quickly scribbled down.

'Why did you two call it that?'

'Well, Helene wasn't like the others. She hated me before she ever laid eyes on me. I was afraid of her. The boy was at a riding camp in Sweden, Mrs Andersen was ill, and I had been utterly alone for a week. I sat here, racking my brains over what could be done. After all, there are no reference books for such situations. I wanted to put an end to it. To get her out of our lives. I couldn't sleep, so I drank all the more. As I sat here, I found myself staring at that American encyclopaedia of his on the bottom shelf. I had never realized that books could be so heavy. I stuffed all fifteen volumes into two suitcases. My plan was to take all of his belongings to her place, seeing as he had moved in there. Why I started with the encyclopaedia, I have no idea. It would have made more sense to haul his clothes over there first,

Vilhelm's Room

but what woman is sensible in a moment like that? Sobbing with rage, I set off to Vester Voldgade, you know the place, lugging a suitcase in each hand. And who do you think ended up dragging them all the way back? Helene and I, trailing after Vilhelm.'

Lise suddenly fell silent and let her hands, which had accompanied her story with lively pantomime, sink back into her lap. Vera hadn't laughed along. She found nothing amusing about the incident. But for Lise, this was the first time since that dreadful day that she had encountered another adult who had known Vilhelm – though, of course, it was an entirely different Vilhelm. When it came to him, there were only two kinds of women: those who were utterly obsessed with him and those who despised him.

Vera set the notepad aside. If it hadn't been her job to find this strange woman sympathetic, she probably wouldn't have. There was no connection between this restless creature who lived entirely in moods of her own making and the sweet, tender love poems that had once comforted Vera and so many other heartbroken girls. Vera felt deceived and had to resist the urge to thrust something sharp into Lise's body. At the same time, she made a quiet note to herself: *She looks like a guest in her own home.* The two of them smoked so heavily that a fog engulfed them. The night's blue fingers groped at the windows, and Vera, who rarely drank, felt tipsy. Now the noise in the background was so faint it sounded like a mouse scurrying within the walls.

'Who've you got in there?' Vera asked with a smile, jerking her thumb over her shoulder.

'Kurt,' said Lise. 'He doesn't like strangers.'

'Are you afraid I might steal him?'

To Vera's surprise, Lise blushed and held out her splayed fingers as if to inspect her nails. Then, softly, she said:

'That's what I asked Mille on the phone the day before I was admitted. At least, that's the expression I used. I said, "You don't plan on stealing him, do you?"'

'What did she say?'

'She said, "Well, he's not a teddy bear!"'

Then Lise's face crumpled, like that of a child subjected to an overwhelming injustice. She wept silently, not bothering to wipe the tears from her cheeks. Vera knew Lise had a habit of inserting herself into Vilhelm's extramarital affairs. For about a year, the three of them made no secret of going out and coming home together, and Vera had actually thought it rather clever of Lise. But it was also madness. Her earlier uneasiness returned. All these closed doors. The heavy, faded drapes, the bland smell of a halted life that could not be resumed. She pulled herself together.

'How's Tom?' Vera asked. 'What a sweetheart. I remember when he came by the office once – he must have been about nine or ten – and said he wanted to speak to his father. When we asked who his father was, he said, "He's the one who tells everyone what to do", and we knew exactly who he meant.'

Lise laughed and dried her tears. Then she stood up and smoothed her dress, indicating that the audience was over. It occurred to Vera that Lise must be 'media-literate', a term she reserved for difficult cases. Regardless, it was time to leave. There was something about this house that made her both frightened and irritated with herself. She longed for flowers, perfume, mirrors.

'One last question!' She snatched up her notepad before getting to her feet.

'Do you still believe in true love?'

'I believe in hope,' said Lise, who knew it made for a strong closing. 'And I can't stand the truth!'

Just as they were about to shake hands, the doorbell rang. They both jumped, and in Vilhelm's room the muffled sounds abruptly stopped.

'Would you be so kind as to open the door for me?' Lise whispered.

Vilhelm's Room

Vera couldn't find the light switch in the hallway, but she found the doorknob. On the doormat stood a hideous old woman, extending a gnarled hand. Then the stairwell's light went out too, leaving only a musty smell like unwashed bedding and a wheezing voice:

'Could you spare a cup of flour?' it croaked.

Right behind Vera was the door to Kurt's room, and that was what the woman's eyes were trained on. Vera could feel it, even though she couldn't see anything. She mumbled that she didn't have any flour, but the abomination cut her off:

'Tell the lady,' she rasped impatiently, 'that her dear lodger will have to fetch his own suitcase. I've reported him to the civil registry office, so he'll need his papers sooner or later.'

'I have no idea what you're talking about!'

Vera slammed the door shut just as Lise switched on the lights in the hall. As she stood there, framed in the doorway to the living room, Vera finally glimpsed the sweet girlishness she had sought in vain while they were sitting across from each other. If she were so inclined, she thought in passing, she would be attracted to someone like Lise.

'What was that about?' she asked, reaching for her coat on the hook.

Something darted past her, and suddenly Lise was holding a cat in her arms. It gazed at Vera with cold, blue eyes. Lise scratched its chin and pressed her cheek into its glossy fur.

'Just the poor old widow from upstairs,' she said absentmindedly, 'She's not right in the head. That's all.'

The same fate would await Lise soon enough, Vera thought as she looped her scarf – a purple one – around her hair and waved down a cab. She would put her whole soul into this interview. She would insist it made the front page, and surely her editor couldn't disagree, since he had demanded an exclusive.

9

When Kurt heard the old hag's threat, his knees began to buckle, yet in that moment the broken bond between them was fatefully reforged. Visions he had believed erased from memory's eternal blackboard reappeared – flickering, vague and tantalizing, laced with an ashen, catastrophic scent, as if his grim fate had not yet forgotten him, the man with no identity who was aware of his own existence only insofar as it influenced those around him. He acted only when he felt threatened, like a predator that doesn't hunt unless hungry. Seated at Vilhelm's desk, he found himself holding a passbook for a savings account with a balance of thirty-five thousand kroner. He had discovered it wedged between two books on the shelf below the windowsill, and in reaching for it, he had accidentally knocked several hefty tomes on national economy to the floor. That was the sound Vera had heard.

The passbook was in Vilhelm's name, and Kurt had initially intended to give it to Lise. Now, he found himself wondering why Vilhelm had hidden this money from his wife. Their relationship seemed steeped in mutual distrust. When Kurt had cautiously inquired about her finances, she had told him that Vilhelm had no idea how much money was in her bank account. He noticed that Vilhelm had deposited this money in a different bank. Then, almost absent-mindedly, he pulled open a drawer and slipped the passbook beneath a stack of photographs of girls in various stages of undress, all very fair and slim, and so similar that only after studying them closely did he realize that they were not the same person. In one of the pictures, the eyes had been gouged out. After hiding the passbook, he stood up and began to pace across the floor, half-listening to Lise and Vera's chirping farewells. He hooked his thumbs into the armholes of his waistcoat, as that was what the boy had told him his father always did when he wanted to lend weight to his words.

Vilhelm's tailored clothes fit Kurt significantly better than the late Mr Thomsen's had. Only the trousers were a little too short. There were five suits in total, but the boy preferred him in the summer suit his father had been wearing the last time he saw him. Despite Kurt's limited powers of observation, two things did not escape his notice: They were completely indifferent to him, yet they could not do without him. They asked no personal questions but treated him with a discreet politeness and regard that pleased him, though he did not feel the need to question the motives underlying their conduct. Previously, the only threat to his sense of security had been the possibility of Vilhelm's return. It was this fear that drove Kurt to read his diaries (they were shelved between two bulky bookends the boy had crafted in woodwork class) with that particular mental thrift found solely among artists and criminals – taking in only what he needed, nothing more. And the man whose room he lived in, whose bed he slept in, whose clothes he wore and whose movements and habits he imitated with the boy's help; this man, whom he had never seen, seeped deeper and deeper into him, replacing the dreamy haze of his soul with the sharp, brutal contours of a person who ruthlessly followed his instincts yet still managed to make something of himself. Lise hadn't made the demands of Kurt that he had feared upon reading her advert. At first, it had been a relief, but gradually an indistinct longing crept in, only tempered by the boy's companionship.

When they were alone, Kurt could tell him stories about himself, conjuring up a version of a Vilhelm some twenty years younger: a youthful, daring figure they could freely invent since neither had ever known him.

Only when Kurt set his anecdotes in America did Tom laugh at such a barefaced lie, and perhaps the truth wouldn't have interested him anyway. But it was an indisputable fact that before people had stopped expecting anything of Kurt, he had been sent off to Los Angeles, where a distant relative owned a wine company. This relative had tolerated him patiently, even when he proved to be a lousy salesman who preferred slumping over a beer in one of the thousand identical dive bars inevitably found next to highway gas stations rather than being ignored by shopkeepers who always cheerily served the customer first before permitting him, with an irritated grunt, to place his brochures on the counter. The relative had put him up in the attic of his mansion, next door to famous movie stars and screenwriters, but regrettably, right above the bedroom of his eighteen-year-old daughter, who was a bratty spectacle of beauty and intelligence. Kurt had impregnated her in a fit of virility of which he later had no recollection. His only memory was of being so drunk that he had struggled to find the keyhole, despite the fact that it was framed by freshly polished decorative brass.

In the days that followed, the beauty began to send him very telling looks across the dinner table, and one evening she pressed herself against him in the attic's dark corridor, whispering as she ran her fingers through his thick hair that he was her big, naughty boy. It was extremely uncomfortable, and he considered finding another place to live, for even then aggressive girls terrified him. But her strange behaviour had already subsided by the time her father summoned him to his lavish private office one day, bade him take a seat and proceeded to viciously

Vilhelm's Room

berate him because this deed, of which Kurt knew nothing, had sullied the family's honour and worse. The gravity of the situation only dawned on him later that evening when the girl's mother spelled it out, telling him to go back where he came from as soon as possible. Too shocked to think clearly, Kurt had accepted a one-way ticket on the *Queen Mary*. The black chauffeur had escorted him on board with a knowing smirk and handed him a wad of cash, of which only ten dollars remained by the time Kurt again set foot on Danish soil.

During the voyage, Kurt brushed up on his half-finished law degree and came to the conclusion that, going forward, he'd need to hide his presence from the authorities. It proved easier than expected. The entire episode seemed distant and unreal, as though it had taken place on another planet, yet ever since, he had harboured a not insignificant fear of alcohol. When he moved downstairs, he had deliberately forgotten his suitcase. It contained all his personal documents – birth certificate, passport, an American driving licence and a sizeable collection of his business cards, each bearing very different yet equally impressive titles: executive director, editor, export manager and author. Such existences are exceedingly common, though they are usually found only in dive bars in the early morning hours, where they seem to arise from the noxious stench that clings to those who lead erratic, anomalous lives.

Indeed, that is how Lise perceived him, remarking with a certain cold, professional curiosity: the Earth swallows them after six or seven years. The rain washes them away, the walls absorb them or a seemingly insignificant disease takes them out, defenceless as they are. But there was something unique about this decided loser which her selfishness and personal misfortune prevented her from seeing. Something that Vilhelm the Runaway had not managed to suppress in Kurt the Good's mind: compassion. It rose in him like nausea in the evening when she spoke of her despairing, homeless love with that quiet, dusty voice that always played the same tune. Only the boy could distract her from this endlessly recurring subject, namely why Vilhelm had left her and how, had she been more vigilant, she might have prevented it. However, Tom usually retreated to his room after they had eaten. There stood the television, the radio and the stereo system his parents could never stand to be in the same room with. Besides, whenever all three of them were together, a slight tension would surface. Lise and Tom would then inevitably give in to the urge of two conspirators to exclude a third. They did so by reminiscing about shared memories of Vilhelm – incidents they had always laughed about behind his back, for just like the young man who had now crept into the lining of his clothes, Vilhelm had a tendency to fly into a rage whenever his actions unintentionally amused others. Lise and Tom thrust these anecdotes upon Kurt with such enthusiasm that they were constantly interrupting each other.

This time, it was the story of when Vilhelm drank himself sober. Yes, he had the habit of lying in bed for days on end, gulping down whisky or rum while he dedicated himself to dramatic readings and prolonged bouts of crying, for which he demanded an audience. Lise and Tom would take turns sitting by his side, and when Mille came along, it had been such a blessing how readily she took over. She seemed capable of going without sleep indefinitely. Then, on one such occasion, Vilhelm's secretary called – he was due to give a speech in English for some prominent American at the Students' Union. Wobbly and grey-faced, with deep black bags under his eyes, he staggered into the living room in nothing but his underwear and collapsed into a chair. He looked as though he needed his stomach pumped immediately. He was no longer dangerous or unpredictable. He even winked cheekily at the boy as he snapped his fingers and ordered, 'Run along and get me six beers, I need to drink myself sober!' He lined the bottles up in front of him and removed the caps with stiff movements, then proceeded to empty them one by one, peering into each beforehand as if to make sure they contained the advertised quantity. Afterwards, he let out a loud belch and declared, 'Mark my words, in a couple of hours, I'll give the best English speech that man will ever hear in this country. Not that it matters, he's as dumb as an oyster.' He said that about all men. Only a few women, in his view, possessed a certain kind of intelligence – if they cared to use it, that is.

From the bathroom, they heard him moaning and cursing his wretched existence, beseeching the heavens, then loudly announcing his intention to completely change his life, and finally, with the door left slightly ajar to make sure they heard him, he bellowed the unspeakable torment of his soul: 'I'm a sick man, a tired man, a man full of sorrow.' Half an hour later, he was ready to go, or rather, to drive, for he never went anywhere on foot. Lise, unbidden, had called a taxi. He looked dapper. Smelling of soap and cologne, the puffiness of his eyes carefully concealed by his spectacles, he was dressed in his finest ministerial attire, which he never wore any more. Later, he told them that upon arriving at the office, he had asked his secretary for a large glass of cognac. After downing it, he wrote his speech (by hand, he never used a typewriter), and then went to the event where he delivered it almost without glancing at his script. The next day, it was printed in the paper.

As they recounted these stories to the ever-solemn Kurt, stories that had practically become myths and legends, they acted them out with their entire bodies. They leapt up and plopped down, they swayed across the room, they burst into tears without shedding any and roared like madmen, radiating a joy they could revisit for the rest of their lives. But they knew not to stage such performances too often in the presence of a third person. They were merely reminding Kurt, a little facetiously, a little deliberately, and a little tenderly, of their ability to extract amusement from even the most atrocious situations, and without uttering a single word they told him where he stood: on the outside, looking in. And just as his nostrils began to flare and his fists to clench, they stopped. The boy vanished so abruptly it was as if he had fallen through a trapdoor in the floor, and Lise looked at Kurt with adorably apologetic eyes and said, 'It's obviously mad, but rather impressive all the same, isn't it?' Until then, she had tactfully yet consistently avoided any physical contact with him, but when Vera left that evening and he hesitantly stepped into the living room, she had rushed over and taken his hands, her eyes sparkling just as they must have done, once upon a time, when Vilhelm came home.

'Could these hands strangle an adult?' she asked with a smile.

'You're drunk,' he replied politely.

'And your hands are very cold.'

She let go of them with a shudder, as if they were two slippery, slimy fish. Kurt muttered something about a headache and quickly retreated to the whispering silence of Vilhelm's room. Uneasy and confused, he glanced around. Everything his eyes landed on seemed to issue an imperious command. He looked down at his long, slender hands with their badly cut nails. Upstairs, in his suitcase lay a complete manicure set, bought in California just like the suitcase itself, which was made of canvas and had worn leather corners. If the old woman had been telling the truth about reporting him, he would claim that he had only been in the country for the six months he had lived with her. His failure to register as a resident with the local authorities was merely a careless oversight. But the old hag's words still rang in his ears, and he couldn't get rid of them. He had used Lise as a shield against the past, yet the sound of Mrs Thomsen's voice had been enough to bring it all back: that hissing of hers, wrapped around other words, growing louder and louder, drawing closer – until it fell silent, just before the eruption.

In the dim light of the antiquated chandelier, with its many insect-flecked glass shades, the indeterminate spots on the neglected parquet floor looked like splatters of dried blood. Kurt was afraid. His fingers trembled slightly as he opened one of the diaries to a random page. It read: 'When we came home with that damned encyclopaedia, I heard the bitches screeching and bickering while I was in the kitchen looking for something to drink. When I rushed in, they were scratching at each other's faces, drawing blood. In my drunken state, I cheered them on, and though Lise came off worse, my sympathy lay with Helene. I felt sorry for her. Despite my notorious cynicism, I often feel sorry for other people. Lise, however, I have never felt sorry for, except in the early years of her addiction, when I bore no blame for her suffering. It's because she is the only person in the world I consider my equal. That day, I forced her to wash the blood off Helene's pale face, stripped of make-up from all her crying. I made her brew coffee and serve it to us. When she poured it for me and her battered face came close to mine, I wanted to pull her close and beg for forgiveness. But she enjoyed this humiliation, and countless others like it, this confounding woman, whom I, also in a metaphorical sense, have only ever penetrated superficially. Beyond that, one hits against something sacred and innocent, like in someone who is chronically pregnant. A locked door not even she can open. I think it's the curse of talent; one is completely shut out, and one hates her for it. She is so ignorant, so helpless, she cannot even fill out a postal order. And yet she possesses something I cannot take from her. That, I suppose, is why I haven't run away screaming, for she is certainly a nightmare to live with. I must have fallen asleep on the sofa, because when I woke up, Helene was gone. Lise was watching me, and it looked like her eyes were bleeding too. Tenderness and anguish filled me. I stroked her beautiful hair, still as blonde as the day we first met. She buried her face in my lap. We both cried. "My little wife," I murmured. "Our boy must never leave us. He is the anchor that keeps us grounded." Then she lifted her bruised face and looked into my eyes: "After such knowledge, what reconciliation?" she said, quoting Eliot – in a terrible translation, but when would she have learned English? This stoker's daughter, who left school after seventh grade! She leeches off my knowledge, kneads it into something new in her mind and spews it out as exceptional poetry she could never have written without me! I hate her, hate her, and even though Helene is nothing more than a sex toy, she has already given me greater, more refined pleasures.'

Kurt thought of the girl in the photograph whose eyes had been gouged out. That had to be Helene. Very young, heavily made-up, naked, with both hands modestly covering her sex. Then he thought of Mrs Thomsen's talon-like fingers as his own slipped slowly into Vilhelm's underwear. His young body flushed.

Elsewhere lay Vilhelm, sleepless and drunk, rambling on about Lise and the boy. Mille listened patiently. She kissed his salty skin, from his shoulder to his fingertips. She loved him. Even so, she said, 'It was wrong of you to leave them. I shouldn't have made it so easy for you.'

10

Editor-in-chief Harald Fairhair (he was bald except for a few wispy tufts just above his ears, resembling the handfuls of hay fed to snappish horses) read the interview in the paper over his morning coffee, which he always enjoyed in the study because he liked how it smelled of books and antiques, though most of them had been inherited from his wife's dignified family. The piece filled the centrefold, and the headline read: *It's wonderful to be alone!* Harald had come up with it himself. Sliding the paper over to his wife, he said with satisfaction:

'Have a look. Vilhelm won't exactly be amused.'

'She looks good,' his wife remarked, 'for her age.'

'We wanted the kid and her new fellow in the photograph, but it couldn't be arranged.'

The article opened with one of Lise's most popular poems:

> *There are two men in the world*
> *who always cross my path,*
> *one is the man I love,*
> *the other man loves me.*

'Who's the third man?' Vera asked by way of introduction, going on to conjure a 'comforting pipe' in an ashtray alongside a bouquet of 'resplendent winter roses', which the photographer had subsequently needed to procure. She had Lise smile 'sweetly and secretively' at the intriguing question, though the smile didn't reach her 'melancholic, cloudy-grey eyes'. Harald was somewhat dissatisfied with the description and even more so with the fact that the noisy outcome of the advert apparently was not something she wanted to show off.

He looked expectantly at his wife, whom wagging tongues claimed was the paper's de facto editor-in-chief. She poured herself a fresh cup of coffee and sighed softly, as if the silver pot were truly too heavy, as if suddenly everything were too heavy; life, marriage, the years gone by, and the belated fruit of her loins, which they had initially mistaken for a tumour. At her age – and their first, at that!

'The headline is daft,' she said in her quiet, weary voice. 'If being alone was really so wonderful, she wouldn't have placed that ad.'

'The point is,' said Harald, wounded, 'it must be a blessing for any woman to be rid of that cad.'

'Why do you hate him so?'

The lady furrowed her brow slightly as she stirred her coffee, not looking at him. She believed that any display of strong emotion was a sign of impropriety.

'I don't hate him. He just has a unique talent for making me feel like an idiot. Frankly, it's a relief he no longer shows his face at the Union of Editors.'

'So where does he show his face?'

'Not at the paper, in any case. Since he left her, he's mostly been on sick leave. Even so, circulation is still rising. But it won't last. Once the stories about naked girls, the gays and transvestites reach the last bachelor pads in Jutland, it'll all fade away. Then the culture pages will be ours for the taking.'

Mrs Fairhair had heard this speech so many times before that she didn't bother responding. She couldn't be bothered with much of anything, but as she stared out at the magnolia tree – still blooming long past its time, just like her – a sharp, clear thought cut through her pregnant inertia.

'What about,' she said with feigned absent-mindedness, 'asking Lise Mundus to write her memoirs for the paper? About her undoubtedly fascinating marriage? People can't get enough of celebrities' candid confessions, or whatever you want to call it.'

'Not our readers. They'd find it tacky.'

A few hours later, however, her idea had taken root in him as a stroke of genius, hatched entirely by his own brain. He called Lise and had no trouble securing a meeting.

That same morning, she had received a disturbing letter from the tax authorities informing her that she owed fifty thousand kroner in back taxes. The year before last her income had been too high, and no one had told her that she should have requested to spread the payments over several years. She no longer had such a sum in her account. She found the whole matter more dull than concerning. It simply occurred to her that had joint taxation not been repealed, then Vilhelm could never have left her. All misfortune arises from the world changing while one is powerless to stop it. Since Mrs Andersen took care of all the shopping, Lise had lost track of prices. How much did an egg cost? The boy shared one every morning with the cat, and three people happily observed this familiar ritual, full of reverent devotion, as if the orange yolk slid into their own stomachs and granted them a magical power to endure the burden of existence. On this morning, though, the walls sloped inwards and the delicate curtains fluttered as if caught in a sudden gust of wind. Inside the transparent boy squirmed grey worms of dread and decay, and his delightful tussle with the cat, this cruel and affectionate performance that should have been sung or danced, served only to distract from a catastrophe all the more terrifying for being impossible to imagine. In her mind, Lise drew him close, for in the past he had always given her strength. Most likely, the world held no meaning in and of itself, but when everything was so uncertain, one had to assign immense significance to a simple, silly ritual like eating an egg in the morning, just as her mother would make the sign of the cross over the bread before slicing it. Without knowing why.

The boy smiled at her and pressed the napkin to his lips. Mrs Andersen blew out the Advent candle, and Lise regarded Kurt with the same ravenous expression that had startled and repulsed him upstairs at Mrs Thomsen's when she realized he might prove useful. When Lise, with a look of helplessness, handed him the acid-green papers across the table, nothing in his demeanour or voice betrayed how deeply he understood Vilhelm's hatred, which flared briefly in his mind. He merely lowered his heavy eyelids for a second (after noting the numbers), and then, without looking at her, he said:

'You must be able to come to an arrangement with the tax authorities. Or request an advance from your publisher. You keep saying it's their fault.'

Each word was said so politely, as if he held the deepest respect for language.

She did not reply. She had already lost interest in the subject.

For a moment, he looked at his hands, bewildered. They lay limp on the tablecloth like something that did not belong to him, something Mrs Andersen had forgotten to clear away. Then he sought refuge in Vilhelm's bed, where he disappeared into the sallow mists of his twisted fantasies.

When the telephone rang, Lise gave a start, like a train jolting forward after a prolonged stop at a station. She has always lingered too long in all sorts of states, even the most unhappy. And for this aged child, just as for Vilhelm, love is indistinguishable from despair. However, she too had noted the numbers, blunt and unpoetic like a punch to the face. She agreed to have lunch with Fairhair. Only when he mentioned the name of his newspaper did she realize who he was. His nickname had been Vilhelm's doing. And now, as everything began to fall into place in a way both diabolical and delightful, she knew – without being aware of it – that the negotiators were on their way, and that the rabid destruction of Vilhelm's room had begun.

II

Out in the stairwell stood the old witch, clutching the marble lion's helplessly exposed member, which still bore traces of the purple crayon Tom and an accomplice had used to colour it many years ago. Lise was about to slip past her when the croaky remnants of a voice sputtered out between wobbly dentures, halting her escape:

'I spoke to your husband yesterday. I told him the innocent boy has fallen into the clutches of a vile prostitute who has grown too old and lazy to offer himself to those fine gentlemen in the public toilets under Rådhuspladsen, who want good value for their money, same as everyone. And if he doesn't do something to save his son, it won't be long before the police come knocking.'

'What did he say to that?' Lise interjected quietly. For four months, her thoughts have been confined to that final hour up there in the rented summerhouse, like prisoners in those so-called tiger cages that are too small to stand upright or lie down in. Only with words could she break free, and since they refused to come to her, she had to seek them out in the world. Her eyes lingered on the hag's doughy, mildewed face; no doubt, she was half-dead from starvation, Lise thought. She simply registered this, as she did so many other things, with the narrow sliver of consciousness that still formed a kind of sluice for new impressions – for all experiences and observations since the day she had fainted into Mille's arms.

'That he's coming back.'

The words flew from the old woman's lips as involuntarily as droplets of spit. Lise had pried them out because she needed them. She smiled, wanting to say something impossibly sweet, but instead a silence settled between them, like between two sisters who have grown old together and no longer need words to communicate. It's love, thought Lise, astonished, as the woman released her grip on the lion and disappeared up the stairs with surprising nimbleness. Lise thought of her mother. 'You're too ugly,' she had told Lise when she was thirteen, the year she had wanted to go to the ball with her mother and older brother. And now they were all dead, and this was true loneliness: there was no one left to talk to about her childhood. She alone could remember that island of a room, which seemed to hover somewhere between Heaven and Earth and contained the three people who had forever shaped her fate. Would she have loved Vilhelm so much had he not resembled her mother? ('Your problem,' he had once said in his gentlest, most dangerous voice, 'is that you lack literary audacity. Take this line, for example' – and the page with her childlike scrawl, which she had not yet learned to hide before he came home, stiffened and died in his hand as he murdered a poem, a cold corpse shrouded in white lace – 'it falls apart in the middle, at the word "heart" . . .' She stared at him, entranced by such pure evil, such a burning need to jab a probe into the softest, most defenceless part of her. In a fit of shame, she had torn the paper into tiny pieces, all the more bound to him because she was incapable of anger.) All these thoughts raced through her in seconds, summoned by the look in the old woman's eyes: a look like the witch's just before she decides that Hansel is fat enough for slaughter.

Bravely, Lise waded into reality as if into a cold, bottomless pool, where one has no choice but to start swimming. And there they stood – the two negotiators – between the front door and the taxi, staring at her with the shameless curiosity one does not bother to conceal from a woman who's been left and must now, impossibly late in life, fend for herself.

'A word, please, ma'am?' one of them asked.

'Now's not a good time. I have a meeting to get to,' she replied solemnly, for it was a magical phrase she had never used before. She glanced at her wristwatch, unable to make out the time without her glasses. She recognized the two men, who had previously tried to evict them after the union bought the property. Vilhelm used to send them packing fairly quickly by citing some section of tenancy law.

'But perhaps later this afternoon. How is five o'clock?'

'Excellent, Mrs Mogensen. That suits us just fine.'

The two men watched as the car pulled away, looking like a pair of chastised schoolboys. They exchanged looks and collected themselves.

'Soon enough,' said the one, 'she won't even be able to afford a taxi.'

'The question is,' replied the other, 'how long can she afford to stay in the flat? I doubt her husband will cover the rent.'

'Or that other fellow's upkeep! There won't be any room for him in the flat we're offering her. So, actually, we're doing her a favour.'

They both eyed the window of Vilhelm's room, where the curtains were always drawn. Kurt observed them through a gap, oblivious as to who they were. They looked like plainclothes policemen. Earlier that day, Mrs Andersen had gone upstairs to retrieve his suitcase, only to be informed that Kurt could fetch it himself once he paid the six months' rent he owed. Mrs Andersen had passed the message on to Kurt without comment, but to her husband she remarked that she hoped he wouldn't coax the money out of the poor, unsuspecting lady of the house, who had enough worries as it was. And what could possibly be in that suitcase other than a pile of dirty laundry? Judging by Kurt's eagerness to get hold of it, one would think it contained a severed head or something like that.

'We would like you to write a series of articles about . . .'
Harald always began a sentence with the greatest of ease and then let others finish it, rather like people who stammer. Lise had already noticed this while they were discussing what food to order.
'My failed marriage?' she suggested with a smile.
'Precisely,' said Harald, relieved, and his head looked like an egg with a face painted on it. The air between them was charged with sympathy. Coloured lights twinkled in their glasses, and the other diners regarded them kindly. They recognized Lise from the paper, from the naïve advertisement that had made her such easy prey for the first marriage fraudster to come along. It was so amusing and so tragic, and she looked as though she had no idea anyone was watching her.
'It wouldn't be easy,' she said calmly, 'I have the children to think of. And I certainly feel no urge to seek revenge on my husband.'
Only when she spoke those last two words did it occur to her that they were, in fact, still married. She recalled the ease with which their respective divorces had been arranged when the two of them decided to marry. When you're in love, you can tolerate other people's unhappiness far more easily than in a normal state of mind. Who was it that said that if people had never learned to read, very few would fall in love? She composed herself, letting her hair fall across her face as she slipped a bite of something into her mouth. Harald had foreseen a few obstacles, but this job, he thought, was a bloody tough one, and he couldn't help but think of the way his dignified wife's mouth tugged at the corners when he said 'our readers'; as if they were

incubator babies, she liked to say. And this woman, so modestly, almost shabbily dressed, wearing no make-up (there were indeed faint marks from Helene's nails on her face – everyone in the innermost circle knew the story, and now the scoundrel had run away with someone else entirely!), this woman was still exceedingly charming. One felt compelled to protect her, quote poems to her, confide to her that one was not particularly happy either.

'That's not the intention,' he said, refilling her glass. 'You don't have to expose anyone other than . . .'

'Myself?' Lise laughed, for in a way, that was all she had ever done. She rested her elbows on the table and brushed her hair away from her face with her fingertips.

'Yes,' said Harald cautiously, 'but no more than you care to.'

'Do you know him?'

'Of course.' (Does she even know who I am, wondered Harald.) Then, pensively, he added:

'They say he's fat now.'

Startled, he noticed that Lise suddenly looked as if he had slapped her in the face. (Later that evening, he relayed the conversation to his wife. 'How tactless!' she exclaimed. 'It must be hard enough to lose one's husband after so many years, but then to find out that he's eaten like a pig and grown fat while she's grieved herself half to death!')

It was the first real piece of information she had received about Mille's Vilhelm. The shock of it pressed all other words down to the scoured floor of her consciousness. All at once, a chill overcame her, and she felt the weight of other people's stares. Mille's teddy bear was so stuffed with wood wool or foam that its furry belly was about to burst. With tremendous effort she regained her composure.

'How much would you pay for such a series of articles? And how many issues would it span? I've heard readers grow bored if it's more than seven or eight.'

She didn't hear his reply. Money no longer mattered. She could ask Kurt to negotiate with the tax authorities. Instantly, she was gripped by the fear that the old woman might take Kurt away from her too soon. For one should never let one's characters act of their own accord. It's bad enough that, out of sheer impatience to be rid of this Lise, here, in her final book, I basically make her out to be worse than she really is. As she scurries across Rådhuspladsen in the cold wind, dishevelled and red-nosed, it seems as if her flapping hair is trying to break free from her, or, failing that, lift her up over rooftops and spires with the raging storm. She was not made for outdoor use.

And now, we will play out scenes from her inner life, interspersed with certain external events of greater or lesser significance; that remains to be seen. What reason is there, now that Vilhelm has grown fat (i.e. as good as dead), to conceal the fact that he once possessed a body: warm, trembling, sensitive and capable of inflicting terrible harm with the slightest caress? I must grant this odalisque, this gazelle destined to be devoured by the lion (these were Vilhelm's loving words, back when he was still obsessed with her, before his own cruel disappointment at seeing his precious feelings curdle into inexplicable hatred made him spit in her face and call her 'Denmark's oldest teenager'), I must bestow upon this woman a new language, the audacity of which Vilhelm will no longer have reason to question. And once all that is done, she must face her downfall like so many others in this city where people die each day in their lonely caves, unnoticed until the smell begins to bother the neighbours; a barrage of grim fates never written down. We must also reject that set of inane, conventional ideas which even now allow platitudes such as 'I only live for my son', 'It is better to be a widow than divorced', or 'I will never get over this' to lay traps for her sharp mind. These are the words all abandoned women reach for, just as they do the dream of a new husband, but what makes our heroine unique is her choice of a man so dreadful that she can be absolutely certain no one will ever take him from her. Now her mind is open to a flood of epiphanies, yet she does not know the ill-fated ability she has to bring out the very worst in others.

The negotiators were waiting in the living room when she arrived home. Kurt sat opposite them, dressed – at Tom's behest – in Vilhelm's finest pinstriped suit. Without making eye contact or giving them the chance to present their arguments, she agreed, just like that, to move into the widower's flat two doors down to accommodate their silly computer systems, which could only be installed in Vilhelm's room. She cast a brief glance at the floor plan of the new residence: With only four rooms, Mrs Andersen would have less to clean. There would be one for each of them, as well as a living room. The negotiators had already obtained Vilhelm's consent, as it was his name on the lease. Now they pushed it towards her; three typewritten lines that made her blush as if at a crude drawing. Her lips became moist, and her legs shook slightly. It was the bitter joy of giving in, of not mustering the slightest resistance, of so obviously being the losing party. Kurt looked on the verge of speaking, bits of his unfinished law degree bubbling to the surface, but Lise silenced him with a single look, forcing the words back down. She quickly scribbled her signature, then escorted the negotiators to the door with such pointed politeness they were left feeling as though they had been forcibly kicked out.

The world turned inside out like a glove. The direction had acquired purpose. The transformation had begun.

★

> Follow this gripping account of a renowned author whose world is upended when her husband abandons her and their son after 22 years of marriage. Candidly and without rancour, Lise Mundus lays bare the tumultuous events that led to a mental breakdown, a stay in a psychiatric facility, and the bold marriage advertisement she placed in Denmark's biggest newspaper – where none other than her husband is editor-in-chief. Officially, they remain married, but the contentious editor-in-chief has moved to a new address.

A Rift in the Marriage

It's very difficult to pinpoint the exact event that led to our ultimate downfall. Like when children spin a globe with their eyes closed and place their finger on some arbitrary location, an island in the Pacific, for instance, and if this happens enough times, they start to believe that island will play a mysterious role in their destiny. As I revisit my experiences, the projector of memory, that probing antenna of my searching soul, persistently and stubbornly returns to that distant night when Vilhelm vomited in the Minister of Culture's lap. It frightened me, and once fear enters a romantic relationship, it is there to stay. I think: He will never forgive me for this. My parents had just left. The minister with the beautiful silver hair had been comparing his poverty-stricken childhood to Vilhelm's poverty-stricken childhood (they were from the same town), each trying to outdo the other in hardship, until by the end it seemed miraculous that either had survived infancy. My father made some feeble attempts to describe his own even more distant, more impoverished childhood until my mother stopped him with a look and a firm hand placed over his glass of cognac. 'You've had enough, Ditlev,' she said, 'we must be getting home.'

Had she joined in, she might have claimed the title of most miserable upbringing, but she was too offended by my neglect that evening. She reminded me of it periodically, right up until she became senile. She also resented me, quite seriously, for forgetting to bring home the laurel wreath so I could use the leaves in a beef stew. She was referring to the Booksellers' Golden Laurels, a great honour at the time, and I was the first woman ever to receive the once-in-a-lifetime award. Vilhelm had written a thank-you speech for me at the last minute, and as I read it aloud with the photographers' flashes erupting around me, I was overcome by shyness. I had never been at the centre of such a grand celebration, and until the post-ceremony nightcap, I truly hadn't had the chance to check on Vilhelm or my mother. Never mind my mother, whose life had been an unbroken chain of perceived slights, but Vilhelm's feeling of being nothing more than an appendage to his famous wife for several hours, some head of department whom no one found the least bit interesting, would have immeasurable consequences for our marriage. The three dead authors (as in now-dead, like so many others) at our table stared in disbelief at Vilhelm, who continued to vomit even after I had lifted his head from the Minister of Culture's tuxedoed lap and helped him to his feet. The minister got up too and smiled very kindly: 'No matter at all,' he said, 'your husband is simply unwell.' Vilhelm swatted my hand away when I tried to steady him, and it was as if all his bitterness and disgust for life kept gushing out of him, down the carpeted hallway of the Engineers' Association and in the taxi home, into the inner pocket of his hired tuxedo, before he suddenly fell into a snoring stupor, his ashen face covered in vomit right up to his short, stiff eyelashes.

The sun was rising and the birds were singing when we finally reached our empty house in Birkerød. Tom, who was two years old at the time, was sleeping at Mrs Andersen's for the night. I manoeuvred Vilhelm into a chair, but when I tried to help him out of his clothes, he kicked me in the stomach. The heel of his shoe tore my long, white brocade dress, and with it, a tear in our marriage into which others could wedge themselves, whether with the noble intention of mending it or the far easier aim of widening it. I stood there, feeling the same mixture of fear and pity I had felt as a child when my mother used to beat me: fear of being subjected to such violent rage, and pity for the helplessness and despair which fuelled it. 'You'll pay for this,' Vilhelm snarled. 'Dragging me to such a ridiculous farce. All those pompous artists – and to think you'd have been nothing without me! When I met you, you were nothing but a blethering drug addict. You knew nothing of Rilke, Eliot or Proust, and now all you do is plagiarize them.'

'Are you saying you want a divorce?' I asked, terrified.

'No, darling, you won't get off that easily.'

I went to bed but couldn't sleep despite my exhaustion. My bedroom faced the garden. In all my marriages, I had insisted on sleeping alone because my fervent childhood dream of having a room of my own had never left me. From that moment on, I began to study Vilhelm's moods like an explorer navigating hitherto untrodden, perilous lands. Until then, I had assumed he was happy because I was, and when he showed all too obvious signs of unhappiness, it had never occurred to me that I might be the cause. Now I knew: what had been smouldering beneath the surface for so long had erupted into a raging fire, but this realization did not have to be plastered on the walls of my room just yet.

In the days that followed, Vilhelm remained upstairs in bed. Like all our furniture, the bed was a by-product of our failed marriages. We felt decidedly indifferent about owning things. It was a cold spring, and the boiler had given out. It was ancient and no one but Vilhelm could get it to work. If anyone else touched it, the door and grate would fall off and be impossible to put back in place. I had to convince Mrs Andersen that Vilhelm had a high fever, so when she left she took Tom with her, not in the slightest displeased to have him all to herself for a while. Cold and whimpering, the boy would trail after Mrs Andersen from room to room, his hands reaching for the comfort of her apron strings, and I envied her a little for the nurturing warmth she radiated, something I neither possessed nor recalled ever experiencing. I loved the sensitive, fairy-tale-like boy he would grow into (that is, the boy I hoped he would become), but I gladly left the preparatory work to Mrs Andersen.

During those bone-chilling days, we wrapped ourselves in all the warm woolly clothes we owned, and surely the end was in sight, Mrs Andersen said, as her husband was less than thrilled to have a small human bundle crawling into their conjugal bed before the crack of dawn. However, she was also of the firm conviction that as long as a man was fed and had enough clean shirts, he would put up with just about anything. Vilhelm's secretary called, inquiring after the head of department. I was under the impression that he only went to work for her sake. She was an old spinster who lived with her mother and their 'tweety-bird', and Vilhelm often grumbled about having to extricate himself before her mother died. In a fit of gallows humour, I told the secretary that my husband had scarlet fever, and with a horrified gasp she wished him a speedy recovery. My mother called, tartly thanking me for a delightful evening but asked me to spare her next time, as none of those fine folk had deigned to speak a single word to her all night. Still, the Minister of Culture had looked nice, so down to earth. If only I had married him instead of Vilhelm. My mother's ambition as it pertained to my husbands knew no bounds. No doubt she had reproached my poor father for failing to become a minister himself, given that a poverty-stricken childhood was evidently no obstacle.

On the fourth day, I sent Mrs Andersen up to Vilhelm to ask him to relight the boiler. He had always treated *her* well, and after she and Tom had left, he did in fact get out of bed. Hair messy (still streaked with vomit) and eyes wild, he grabbed one of the dining-room chairs and smashed it against the floor because the kindling from the shop was always damp. We were storing the chairs for a friend I hadn't seen in years, and I didn't know what I'd tell her if she came by one day wanting them back. Cursing useless, lazy women, he went down to the basement where his loud tirade continued as if he were fighting a sworn enemy. Once he'd got the boiler going, he came back upstairs in his old, blue bathrobe and sat down across from me (I pretended to be reading the paper), emanating such great waves of danger my heart pounded with fear.

'I must change my life,' he said calmly. 'I am thirty-eight years old and don't want to end up a failure. You despise me, just as your mother despises your father. I've been lying in bed thinking it all over. I intend to consult a psychiatrist.'

I did not protest, though I knew of many marriages that fell apart as soon as a psychiatrist was involved. And besides, I had never truly stood in the way of another person's free will. He had heard of someone highly capable, he said, and would call to make an appointment. His name was Jens Olesen, and he was a proponent of Freud. Vilhelm went upstairs, bathed, and returned a little later in his proper head-of-department uniform, a white handkerchief peeking from his breast pocket. I should have kissed him and said something affectionate, but I was afraid he would push me away. His sexual interest in me had waned since I had given birth to Tom. Yet I had never been jealous of the faceless girls he frequented in the city, though I knew perfectly well that my indifference offended him. In truth, we had long tormented each other in that way, a pastime many indulge in when they know each other too well to be in love and not well enough to find comfort in each other's company.

Perhaps the tear in our relationship would have healed on its own had this damned Jens Olesen not wedged himself into it, widening the rift and assuring Vilhelm that I alone was to blame. He burrowed under Vilhelm's skin, saw through his eyes and spoke through his teeth. It was as ridiculous as it was unbearable. Five times a week, Vilhelm rushed straight from the office to Jens Olesen and then home to me, armed with the ammunition that idiot had supplied him with. After dinner, once Tom was in bed, he would pace the floor, beginning every sentence with 'Jens Olesen says –', and though what Jens Olesen had to say was mostly nonsense, it had a devastating effect on me, much like everything my mother used to say to me when I was a child. Jens Olesen said that a man in Vilhelm's position couldn't be satisfied with sausage and spaghetti slop every Sunday. So immediately, I struck this dish from my meagre culinary repertoire. Jens Olesen said that a man in Vilhelm's position couldn't be satisfied with a wife who wasn't interested in his work. Immediately, I made a point of interrogating him about what he actually did at the office, but *that* wasn't the bloody work Jens Olesen meant. He was referring to the weekly articles Vilhelm wrote for *Finanstidende*. Granted, I had never read a single one. When I finally did, I discovered they were full of quotes from Hørup, whose work I had known since my ex-husband Ebbe's time. (An observation I would wield years later when we had mastered the art of hurting each other; for now, we were still just amateurs.)

Furthermore, Jens Olesen said that our great love, which was still not entirely dead, was nothing more than 'morbid dependency' built atop a neurotic foundation. That was the final straw. I bought a bottle of whisky, smeared on some make-up and squeezed into my Himmelbjerg dress, which I could still fit. As intended, this stirred the tenderest memories in Vilhelm, and for the first time in a long while he desired me. But even in the midst of our embrace, I felt Jens Olesen's presence, and sure enough: The next day, the prophet declared that I was dull in bed and that a man in Vilhelm's position couldn't be satisfied by a wife

Vilhelm's Room

of such limited sexual imagination. Only then did I decide to rebel against this parasite, whose services, it must be said, were no small financial burden. His bill was soon due, and, as Jens Olesen liked to say, one was doomed to eternal poverty when one bought a house without a krone for the down payment.

I sought advice from Nadja, my psychologist friend, without considering that the more people you involve in your marriage, the worse it gets. Nadja said that if this madness wasn't to end in divorce, I should go to supportive therapy. She knew a psychiatrist who might take me on, although the rumour that I was not entirely right in the head was already widespread among doctors. Psychiatrists are sick and tired of dealing with mentally ill people day in and out; they prefer private patients who don't actually suffer from any serious issues. My psychiatrist was named Højborg. He was a specialist at a hospital in Copenhagen, and that alone made him superior to the awful Jens Olesen. Dr Højborg was roughly a couple of metres tall and had a long, unending face with saggy cheeks. His bulging brown eyes were often despondent, as if carrying the painful experiences of a failed life. But a glint of hope lit in them when I began entertaining him with stories of Mr Olesen's sabotage. Olesen, he explained, was an unpleasant, self-satisfied fellow who did indeed have the irresponsible habit of driving his patients' marriages to the brink of collapse, because he himself was married to a terrible shrew so obsessed with Women's Lib that Olesen had to cook his own steaks and wash his own underwear. Højborg perfectly understood my need for support in dealing with the charlatan. And with that, there were four of us in the marriage.

The next day, I received a letter from the Minister of Culture. He was pleased, he wrote, to inform me that I had been awarded a lifelong grant of two hundred kroner a month. In a postscript, he added: Please give my regards to your splendid husband. Vilhelm believed it to be an underhanded insult. Jens Olesen believed it implied that, despite the evening's embarrassing conclusion, the minister had recognized Vilhelm's unmatched intellect. Højborg believed the minister's words indicated that the vomiting incident was water under the bridge. Højborg also believed that Olesen had subconsciously fallen in love with Vilhelm, and Olesen believed that Højborg was in love with me. We showed them the photograph taken at Himmelbjerget. They examined it as if through a magnifying glass. A charming psychopath, Højborg deemed Vilhelm. A hysterical neurotic, Olesen exclaimed at the sight of me staring at the photographer while Vilhelm stared at me. During all the ferrying back and forth, the picture had been damaged. We sat on the sofa at home, trying to smooth it out. 'We shouldn't have shown it to those two idiots,' Vilhelm said. We looked at each other like children lured into a trap, and before we knew it, we were choking back tears.

The Perils of Love

This madness lasted two years. Light fell where there had once been darkness, but it was a sharp, cold light that killed any genuine emotion within us. We lost the ability to speak to each other kindly and normally, and we begrudged each other even the most innocent joy. Only Tom constituted a narrow zone of neutrality between us. He had started nursery because Olesen believed it was detrimental for him to spend too much time with such a pathological mother, while Højborg believed the boy distracted me from my work. Højborg also said (though I refrained from relaying it) that I had no reason to be grateful to Vilhelm just because he happened to have saved my life. Such life-savers simply had a chronic need to suffer and chose a partner who could best satisfy this need, be it an addict, a drinker, a hunchback or a sadist. Unsurprisingly, they considered theirs a great and selfless love, but it inevitably dissolved into thin air or turned to hatred if the rescue mission succeeded.

Like all psychiatric dogma, this was a gross simplification, but it contained a bitter grain of truth. When, thanks to Vilhelm's furious battle against the all too obliging doctors (whom he mercilessly reported to the medical council), I had somewhat recovered and began to write again, he suddenly did not know what to do with me. Problems lose their appeal once they're solved. This, said Olesen when Vilhelm recounted Højborg's interpretation, was absolute drivel. I had abused Vilhelm's best and most virtuous qualities in the service of a self-centred and pointless cause, and Vilhelm had seen something in me that did not exist. Had I enriched world literature with my trivial prattling? Olesen (who knows what became of him) told his clever patient that I had been dubbed 'the salon pianist of poetry' in a Swedish article, and when my wicked Vilhelm conveyed this to me with sinister delight, I experienced one of those rare seizures I had suffered from as a child. I collapsed as if struck by lightning and awoke in Vilhelm's loving arms. He had carried me to bed and now lay beside me, staring at me with a helpless look in his eyes. 'Never,' he said in his own, Olesen-less voice, 'have I been so cruel to another human being.' But I had also been cruel, I assured him, and we spent a strange, beautiful night outdoing each other in cruelty. I remembered the poems from gymnasium he had once shared with me. One stanza in particular had been quite good, but I hadn't praised him for it, though I remember it to this day: 'Man alone knows he is the stain / Upon the purity he longs to claim.' Vilhelm, whose memory was excellent, recalled the episode too and agreed that my pettiness had prevented me from praising him. Then he admitted that he had sometimes put words in Olesen's mouth, and I admitted that I often twisted Højborg's words of wisdom a bit, too. Our confessions had no end, encompassing all the wrongs we had ever inflicted on others over the years; my husbands, indistinguishable figures I had never seen clearly and had simply divorced when I believed myself in love with someone else. That night, I asked him why he had been so enraged at his wife when he left her and their little girl, whom I had never met. He said something I would later come to experience first-hand, bitterly and without ever fully comprehending it: The people I truly wrong, I never forgive!

I fell asleep with my face pressed into the warm crook of his armpit.

The next morning Mrs Andersen and I tiptoed about, whispering anxiously, as everything that needed to be done was hindered by Vilhelm snoring away in my bed. I had begun writing my first children's book, a commission that was proving difficult, and I couldn't very well disturb Vilhelm by clattering away on the typewriter right beside him. And Mrs Andersen, though pleased with this obvious sign that we were still performing our matrimonial duties, was prevented from 'airing out' the rooms, by which she meant letting in the gust of fresh air that, prior to the discovery of penicillin, had ensured the swift, peaceful deaths of so many by way of pneumonia. I rushed to deliver Tom to kindergarten. His seat was fastened to my bicycle's rear rack, and as we crossed the bridge with the wind whipping around us, he rocked back and forth to tease me, and I had to tell him to sit still. 'You can't tell me what to do,' he shouted triumphantly, 'Olesen says so.' Laughing, I retorted, 'Well, Højborg says you should listen to your mother!'

But as I cycled home, my red headscarf fluttering behind me, I was seized by a premonition of some as-of-yet unknown horror. The house resembled a lump of butter melting under the harsh glare of the sun. Racing past it, I felt as though my heart was being wrung out like a wet rag. Only when I reached Bistrup Forest did I stop, throwing my bike aside as I collapsed onto a bench in the shade, out of breath. I knew something catastrophic had happened in my absence, just like when, as a child, I would reluctantly leave my parents, terrified that they would seize the opportunity to rip each other to pieces. The sky came to my rescue. Grey clouds blurred together and a soft rain fell from the heavens. If Vilhelm was awake when I returned home, I would say, 'I wonder if it will rain all day?' Though I knew that seemingly innocent words are always the most dangerous, we learn nothing from experience, and a burnt child does not, in fact, dread the fire. He was in the dining room, drinking coffee; Mrs Andersen was upstairs tidying. In his hand, he held a letter. His face bore a serene calm, like the Madonna's: a kind of stern piety akin to that of old, rough-hewn saints which compels us to clasp our hands and remember all our unforgivable sins.

'You're going to Russia,' he said. 'With a delegation of three men – two of whom are Social Dem MPs, both nearly a hundred years old. The third is a doctor, a sympathizer from Aalborg. I've looked him up in *Who's Who*. He specializes in varicose veins and was born in 1920. I'm sure you'll have a marvellous time together, seeing as I have no strings to pull with the Russian health authorities. Presumably, you'll both end up in Siberia.'

He said it softly, in a single breath. The night's stark, cruel confessions lurked behind every word, cutting into my soul like a rusty dagger. The rain lashed against the windows in a rage, as if the world itself refused to tolerate our contentment. The meaning of his words didn't sink in. I said:

'I wonder if it will rain all day?'

'Ask the Meteorological Institute.'

And so began the 'Russian Crisis', thus marking the beginning of the end.

Højborg encouraged me to go. It was, he insisted, part of my job. When he heard about my episode, he prescribed barbiturates to prevent a recurrence. Olesen, however, couldn't for the life of him understand why I had to go to Russia. Unless, of course, I could somehow arrange for Vilhelm to come along too. It was scandalous, said the mouthpiece, that the state was squandering funds on such absurd delegations. That same day, Vilhelm received what was apparently a prestigious invitation to write a tribute for the Faxe Limestone Quarry. He was immensely proud, but when he told me, I merely said, 'How interesting. I wonder which critic will review it . . .'

The week that followed was sheer madness – but what had I actually done? Every evening, Vilhelm would sit in the armchair by my bed, as this crisis was something he had to overcome within himself, once and for all. My not going to Russia wouldn't have helped in the slightest. It must have had something to do with his intense jealousy. He read aloud passages from Proust in which a poet explores the nature of jealousy. The object was irrelevant; it could be anyone. Trembling with fear and compassion, I listened to him read. I stared into a soul steeped in bitterness and heavy with sorrows. Amidst it all, he was seized by violent fits of crying, he spat in my face and tore his clothes to shreds. Højborg diagnosed it as hysteria, but Olesen attributed it to his 'Slavic temperament', since Vilhelm's mother was Polish. Olesen even unearthed a Baltic relative, whose existence made Vilhelm feel estranged from the lukewarm Danes, who valued self-restraint above all other virtues. Olesen, ignoring all psychoanalytic conventions, sought out Højborg, whom he believed to be dealing with a case beyond his expertise. Højborg, in turn, accused Olesen of excessive identification with his patient, which he deemed highly irresponsible. In the end, I had no opinion at all. I simply wanted to get away, even if it meant enduring penal servitude in Siberia – not an unlikely outcome, had Hugo not remained loyally by my side in Russia. Hugo was the doctor Vilhelm had looked up in *Who's Who*, and he became my first lover in seven years. He also unwittingly became the catalyst that spurred us to bring our erotic fantasies to life, after which there was no turning back.

Neck-Deep in Love

We were in hell. A few days before my departure, the toilet became clogged, and with it, the septic tank in the garden. Its rusty lid rose up and was shoved aside as if by an underground monster conspiring with our cruel fate. Faeces, toilet paper and other less identifiable waste products floated with almost majestic inexorability across the lawn, and Vilhelm had not, he announced with horrified disgust, taken Denmark's highest civil-service examination to end up neck-deep in shit. Then he undressed and went to bed. Mrs Andersen, who could handle anything so long as 'the neighbours didn't find out', called the old man who had previously dealt with such atrocities, only to be informed that he was dead.

When we discovered that the ramshackle house we had bought was a pig in a poke, we dubbed it 'The House of Usher', after Poe's story – dismal, dilapidated, sallow like the face of someone on their deathbed, and enveloped in toxic fumes. The dentist up on the main street who always behaved as though he himself, and not his patient, was on laughing gas deemed it the ugliest house in Birkerød. And now that it was evidently also a health hazard, Mrs Andersen took Tom home with her and declared that she and the boy would stay away until I returned from Russia. Thus, our life lost its last semblance of normalcy. Vilhelm ordered me to buy beers and whisky from the grocer while he stuffed himself with the meprobamate that Olesen, to Højborg's dismay, had prescribed him. Anxiety and old guilt tore loose from the fragile moorings in my mind as I realized the truth in Højborg's claim: Had I chosen Vilhelm from a hundred thousand suitors, I could not have found a person more like my mother. You can twist and turn as much as you like, change your surroundings, travel to another continent; you will still end up right where you started, and nothing can ever erase your earliest influences. Later, Vilhelm told me he had felt as if the ground were opening beneath his feet when I left him for fourteen days. We had never voluntarily been apart for so long. Even so, I have never fully grasped the depths of terror and rage he was plunged into. All I know is that the seed of his intense and, to outsiders, incomprehensible hatred for the arts and artists was planted in those days when I sat stone-still, absorbing the sounds that descended from upstairs, not without a certain bitter triumph which likely resembled what my poor mother felt when, on account of some trifle, she employed her dreaded silent treatment, prompting my father and me to cling to her, each of us shouldering the blame for her life's misfortune. Meanwhile, my brother, ill-suited for this brutal game, made himself scarce until the storm had passed.

Mumbled Latin prayers dripped down through the stained ceiling, interspersed with a grating song:

> *My father was a friend of the Russian czar,*
> *My mother, a dearly departed star,*
> *My darling Olga, a love so true,*
> *beneath skies of heavenly blue.*

His secretary called; something about the Faxe Limestone Quarry. I found myself answering in a small, polite voice, 'Unfortunately, my husband has lost his mind.' She let out a neighing sound. 'You are terribly amusing, Mrs Head of Department,' she said once she had caught her breath, 'but the managing director is quite insistent on speaking with your husband, if at all possible?' Vilhelm thundered: 'If it's that varicose vein specialist, tell him you reek of shit.' Quietly, I replaced the receiver. I decided not to go to Russia, skilled as I am in decisions that require nothing but passivity. My worries crawled like white tapeworms up a rickety ladder of grim humour: This is what it had come to, this is how low we had sunk. Yet my despair held a shred of sordid pleasure. I imagined people holding their noses as they walked past in the sunshine. 'Say your prayers, poor peasant on the nightly path.' My anxiety had not diminished, but I began to observe it as something outside of myself. Then my mother rang:

'Lise,' she exclaimed, 'I've had a brilliant idea. Your father will soon be eligible for a pension, but we won't be able to make ends meet until I qualify for one as well. Then, like a bolt of lightning, it struck me: Your Minister of Culture should have no trouble getting your father a job as a museum attendant. Won't you ask him? That way, I'd also be spared having him underfoot all day.'

There was no point in objecting to my mother's schemes, which had only grown more absurd and more crude since I had risen into higher social circles. In the back of my mind, I thought: This will amuse Vilhelm one day.

'I'll be sure to, if the opportunity arises,' I assured her.

'Such a lovely man, that Bomholt,' said my mother. 'Is he married?' (In her mind, she had already married me off to him. She no longer considered Vilhelm worth holding on to after he refused to paint their allotment hut. Her sister's son-in-law had painted theirs; he was a caregiver at a psychiatric hospital. Vilhelm had remarked that it was an odd request, given that their own son was a house painter.)

'Yes, he's married,' I said. 'His wife was there too, seated at another table.'

'What a pity. But you'll remember to ask him, won't you?'

I promised. Vilhelm had fallen asleep, but even his deafening snores carried a threat. Guilt and insight welled up in me; it dripped down through the ceiling from this person I had somehow wronged. I had locked all his wisdom and talent in a box and hidden it where no one, least of all him, would ever find it. And now that damned Olesen had managed to uncover it and was handing it back to Vilhelm. This was dangerous. I didn't need an ambitious man; my own ambition was enough. In the blink of an eye, Vilhelm's admiration for me had turned into a poisonous blend of hatred and envy. Only a miracle would stop him from striking where I was most vulnerable: my artistic self-confidence, which had never been robust. It required constant validation from others; I was a perpetual schoolchild who could not thrive without the teachers' praise. Good reviews pleased me only insofar as they confirmed that I had once again deceived my critics – though how, I did not know. Things between Vilhelm and me started to deteriorate dramatically when I took our marriage for granted. In the eyes of my girlfriends – Vilhelm had long since driven away the few male friends I once had – but in the eyes of those invaluable women, I had long been seen as someone who put up with anything, while in truth, I – not unjustifiably, at the time – saw Vilhelm's benders and infidelity as an homage to me.

I don't know what would have happened if Nina and Gunnar hadn't turned up out of the blue. She and I had shared a chapter of our youth, and she had earned Vilhelm's lifelong devotion when, during one of his self-imposed periods of bedrest, she had single-handedly waged war on the blasted boiler and lit it without resorting to smashing chairs. Vilhelm possessed the endearing quality of never forgetting those who had once come to his aid, even if the favour was scarcely acknowledged or remembered by the benefactor. Nina, who was married to a forester I had only met a handful of times, regarded Vilhelm as one of fate's oddities. When he heard them ringing the doorbell, he bellowed something about not letting anyone into this damn shithouse. I shouted back that it was only Nina, which was met with silence. Unperturbed, Nina simply asked how I could stand the crazy bastard. I filled her in on the faecal affair – it was late afternoon and still light out – and she promptly sent Gunnar out into the garden to tackle the situation with some mystifying tools left behind by the dead old man. Meanwhile, she conjured a meal from the refrigerator's ample provisions, and just as the table was laid, Vilhelm strode into the dining room, freshly showered, clean-shaven and dressed in his head-of-department attire. He greeted Nina warmly and nonchalantly but did not look at me, nor did he address me once the rest of the evening. This was no reconciliation, merely a temporary ceasefire. When the ever-helpful Gunnar returned after an hour-long struggle with the septic tank and the seepage well, which were never in working order at the same time ('a symbol of my life's adversity', Vilhelm used to say), he was lavished with gratitude. After inquiring at length about the weather in Southern Zealand, Vilhelm, his whisky-and-meprobamate-reddened eyes concealed behind tinted reading glasses, was clearly racking his brains for a way to make conversation with a forester. Then, very politely, he ventured:

'Have you ever shot a poacher?'

A slight tug appeared at the corners of Gunnar's mouth, but some instinct for self-preservation kept any of us from bursting into laughter.

The next morning, I took a taxi to the airport. Like a thief, I sneaked out the door with my suitcase in tow, its contents betraying a complete ignorance of Russian weather at that time of year. We had been invited to celebrate the fortieth anniversary of the revolution, though the rationale behind the peculiar composition of the delegation has remained a mystery to me. The two elderly gentlemen looked as if they wouldn't even survive an outing to Husum. On the plane, Hugo the sympathizer, with whom I already shared a kind of otherworldly bond, draped a paternal arm around my shoulder. With a contented sigh, he remarked:

'It doesn't matter where you're going, just as long as you're leaving home!'

But I hadn't left home. The fear of Vilhelm had taken hold of me like rot in a tree, binding me to him more strongly than love ever had.

I had swallowed five of Højborg's seizure pills, washed down with copious amounts of cognac, which we drank all the way to Moscow. Hugo confessed that standing on Red Square would be the fulfilment of a lifelong dream of his, and I recalled that I had once joined the Communist Party because a girlfriend told me that in Russia you could ride the streetcar for free. I had never withdrawn my membership, though it had probably been revoked for non-payment of dues. In my drunken state, I asked Hugo, who was soft and round like a rubber ball, whether I still smelled of shit. Affectionately, he tucked my hair behind my ear and said:

'I don't care how you smell. I'm just glad you're here. What would I have done on my own with those two buffoons?'

They both vomited throughout the flight into bags provided for that purpose, but that didn't deter them from repeatedly shooting us looks of indignation. A sentence from a short story by Dorothy Parker came to my mind, about a woman's descent into the abyss: 'Oh please, God, please keep her always drunk.' And for the next fourteen days, I was.

12

The Saturday morning Lise's first article was published, Mille realized she was not happy. And although this realization erupted in her like a volcano, she remained composed, flipped the toast and removed the tea cosy from the pot as Vilhelm didn't like it too hot. She sat at the oval table she had inherited from her late grandmother, on a velvet-upholstered chair adorned with cross-stitch embroidery sewn by her still very much alive mother, and stared at the elaborate four-poster bed in the darkest corner of the spacious room. It represented her entire share of the marital property following the dissolution of her marriage. She had sewn the striped chartreuse cretonne drapes herself and hung them on big, rattling curtain rings.

From behind the drapes came loud roars and delighted squeals, incited by Vilhelm's newspaper-reading, which today featured Lise's first tell-all. As usual, Mille, well-rested after a good night's sleep, had laid out that day's papers on top of the duvet; Vilhelm claimed that only the smell of fresh ink could dispel the adrenaline built up in his blood overnight. This morning, he had asked her to wake him as soon as the newspapers were delivered, because Lise's series had been heavily publicized, even in his own paper. Amused yet infuriated by the advert's claim of 'a long unhappy marriage', he had scoffed to Mille, who the hell did she think she was? It had indeed been unhappy for him, but hadn't he been the one to save her life? He had recited many a Hail Mary, praying for her sound sleep even in those days when he couldn't look at another man or woman without resenting them because no one was keeping them up at night. As a lapsed Catholic, he still returned to his childhood faith in times of crisis. And one day – still to come – he would once again go to confession, for there was always time to repent between the stirrup and the ground. He had been curious about the interview, and had noted the size of the print run – proof that Lise still made for good copy. He read her article aloud to Mille twice, particularly amused by the fact that Fairhair and other dimwits, including several of his own employees, would believe this to be a lethal blow. Lise was the only one who truly knew him, and she would never expose him in such a spiteful way. Only dilettantes were vindictive and mean, true artists were not.

It was during this rant that Mille realized she was no longer happy. Pragmatic as ever, she moved about in the stylish chequered housecoat she had sewn herself, put the kettle on, laid the table and switched on the toaster. Meanwhile, for the first time in six months, she listened inwardly and heard only a resounding emptiness she could not put into words. Mille thought and dreamed solely in pictures. One of the flat's cramped, impractical rooms is full of her finished and unfinished canvases, and whatever she paints with her tiny silk brushes, it always ends up looking like the starry constellations of liquorice pastilles that little girls stick to the backs of their hands with spit. Over a year ago, Vilhelm had cast a single glance at them and exclaimed in dismay: Good God, they're not half bad! It was the first time he made her cry. And since then, she has not painted and he has not set foot in the room. Nor does he allude to its existence, for he knows full well that he trespassed on her secret dreams that day, and what would he do without Mille? Now his deep, comforting voice swells from behind the curtain of their wide bed:

> *Love is a gypsy child,*
> *it has never, never known a law,*
> *If you don't love me, I love you,*
> *but if I love you, be on your guard!*

It's the 'Habanera' from *Carmen*, which he sang and hummed incessantly that summer, ever since he came across a book about Bizet at the summerhouse. Mille doesn't know this, and she would never be able to guess it. Suddenly, she knows nothing about this man for whom she has done so much he can no longer function without her. She is like a matron of a medieval castle who strides through the halls with heavy keys jangling from her belt and deep pockets filled with needles and threads of every size and colour. No longer does Vilhelm find missing buttons on his shirt or two mismatched socks paired together; though Mrs Andersen took care of the laundry, she left the sorting to Lise, who could write tirelessly for hours on end but found even the smallest domestic effort so tedious it made her nauseous and clammy-handed. Mille had attended domestic science classes in the provincial town where she grew up, and when Vilhelm calls at three in the morning to report that he'll be arriving shortly with a few friends, she welcomes them with midnight snacks, cold beers, and a face as radiant and alert as had she just enjoyed a full ten hours of uninterrupted sleep. She is an invaluable asset for 'a man in his position'; Vilhelm chuckles loudly at the phrase, thinking of Olesen, the closeted homosexual he had relied on during the Russian Crisis. Had Lise only stayed home, he says to Mille for the umpteenth time, I'd never have left her!

Mille is fed up with hearing about the Russian Crisis, but for the first time she refrains from replying when he grants her the rare courtesy of speaking to her before noon. She pours tea with a slightly unsteady hand, and Vilhelm notes that when she is offended, her broad, dependable face resembles that of a horse. A look of sad forbearance settles over it, and one is tempted to pat her muzzle and offer her a manger of oats. The comparison would amuse Lise, but now he'll have to keep it to himself. One cannot argue with Mille. When he tries to provoke her, she dissolves into tears and retreats to the farthest corner of the four-poster bed, where she sobs, raggedly and inconsolably, until exhaustion overtakes her, and she falls asleep like a child. Without looking up from his paper, he reaches for the slice of toast Mille has buttered for him. He studies the photograph of Lise and is overwhelmed by tenderness. How much hatred had he squandered on this woman, who possessed something that could not be taken from her? No one understood that, least of all this specialist doctor's daughter, who, upon witnessing one of their glorious quarrels for the first time, had fled in a panic, jumped into the little Fiat her father had bought her and driven home, resolved never again to attempt to save their marriage. How they had laughed when she telephoned the next day and said: 'I'm just not used to that sort of thing. When Mum and Dad fought, they always went into the library.' Neither Lise's parents nor his had a library in which to settle their disputes. Soon, Mille will drive him to the office (he has never bothered to renew his licence), so it would be highly inconvenient to provoke an episode of weeping. Instead, he says:

'It was her brilliant prose that brought me back to her when I was living with Helene. She wrote me the most captivating letters . . .'

'Not any more. The interview made it sound as though she's found someone new.'

'Nonsense,' snapped Vilhelm, whose good mood always

rested on the flimsiest foundation. 'If she had, the whole press would know by now.'

He stood up so abruptly the bow-legged chair toppled over. Leaving the bathroom door open, he sang loudly, but without joy:

*My girl is fair as amber,
like Denmark's golden wheat . . .*

But for once, Mille isn't listening. His arsenal of torment is quickly exhausted, its variations few and unimaginative. His intention is to remind her of the time his first wife, Agnete, heard him sing those lines one morning and exclaimed: Now I know who you're in love with! And perhaps he also wants to make Mille feel sad that she is by no means 'fair as amber'! Given how remarkably easy it is to use the threat of such abuses to keep someone right where you want them, it's surprising more people don't do it. Something horrible dawns on Mille: She is no longer in love with him. It's horrible because now she must ask herself why she is still with him. Sitting behind the wheel with him in the passenger seat, she asks herself the question for the first time in two years. Inside her, glaciers calve, molten lava erupts into the sky, and she wonders whether she'd feel anything at all if, instead of slowing the car down, she ran right over that confused old man crossing Rådhuspladsen?

Vilhelm disappears into the office, hands in his coat pockets, not looking back. From behind, it occurs to her that his back looks hunched and rigid like a tortoise shell and, for reasons she cannot explain, evokes a memory they do not share. It was almost a year ago. She had been having lunch with Lise at the Glyptotek café, and as always they were talking about Vilhelm. Mille said: 'I don't recognize him in anything you're saying. I mean, he's such a kind man!' Good God, now she understood

Lise's shock at her choice of words. But at the time, she had meant it. He had helped her with rent and the phone bill, and while she was not a calculating person, it had meant something to her. In the months before she met Vilhelm, she had been in a difficult spot. She had rented a flat believing that her lover, also employed at *Hus og Hjem*, would move in with her. But when everything was signed and ready, it turned out his wife was pregnant and he couldn't bring himself to leave her after all.

Mille cannot have children. Her infertility stems from a venereal disease her husband passed on to her a dozen or so years ago. He was a musician and an alcoholic and they had been married only three months when he infected her. Though she never held it against him, he couldn't forgive himself for the repercussions. Guilt made him so cruel he would beat her black and blue when he came home in the early morning hours. Her father intervened and forced him to move out. She never saw him again and only officially divorced him when she decided to move in with her fickle ex-lover. Mille considers herself unbound by social convention. In the editorial office, she and Vilhelm had not bothered to hide their relationship, and when he very abruptly resigned, she followed suit out of sheer loyalty. These days she teaches English to secondary-school pupils (she has a gymnasium diploma and studied three languages), because she doesn't want Vilhelm to support her, nor, quite frankly, has he ever expressed any desire to do so. But Mille knows something is wrong when she starts to look inward and discerns a pattern there. It's my damned maternal instinct, she thinks, turning the car key and slipping it into her pocket. Had I had children, there would have been a natural outlet. Instead, it attracts weak and peculiar men.

Vilhelm's weakness is his unbelievable helplessness when it comes to practical matters. And his inability to be alone for even five minutes, except when asleep. Her weakness – she takes the stairs two at a time – is that she doesn't believe she is worth anything. She exists solely through a man's love and dependency – but she didn't necessarily have to live with him. Vilhelm just happened to be there that day in late July, just as she was about to give up entirely and move back in with her parents. There he stood, grey-faced and with a half-empty suitcase in hand. He brushed right past her and sat down in the living room, staring straight ahead, bleary-eyed behind his glasses, and said softly, insistently: 'Here I am, Mille, and I'm here to stay. I never want to lay eyes on that bitch again.' It was then that she realized that he hadn't so much moved in with her as away from Lise. His hatred for Lise was a mystery to her. He had refused to tell her what had happened in that summerhouse she'd never been invited to. She had been forced to call in sick to work. She had been forced to do so regularly – too often, in fact, to make working tenable. Since Lise's advert, Vilhelm had needed her round the clock. And if she wasn't there, he'd call Helene, who was still available despite having a child with someone else, with whom she had lived until he too had left her.

Mille was jealous of Helene, but that child was her insurance against being left (Vilhelm found it idiotic that it hadn't been aborted). Mille and Lise had always agreed that Helene was the root cause of Vilhelm's suffering and only out to bring him down. Wasn't there . . . Mille made the bed and restlessly paced the rooms, looking for ways to add a feminine touch. Vilhelm complained that Lise, sloppy and absent-minded as she was, had never been capable of that. But on second thoughts – she slumped into the living room's only comfortable chair – she was tired of adding such touches. And wasn't it true of all Vilhelm's women that they allowed him to treat them however he pleased and never resented him for it? She retrieved the newspaper with Lise's article from the floor where he had tossed it and studied Lise's defenceless little face. A pleasant sensation enveloped her, like crawling into bed after a delicious meal in good company. But even that was a distant memory. What was stopping her from calling Lise for a chat? Perhaps she would hang up in anger, but it was worth a shot. She would have to do it right away, while the boy was at school and Vilhelm was at work. Almost happy, she crossed the living room and sat down by the telephone. As she lifted the receiver, she noticed that all but two tulips in the Japanese vase were ready for the bin. Attending to such details was one of those feminine touches. She would toss the whole damn bouquet.

13

It was Kurt who – most reluctantly – answered the telephone. It stood on the sideboard in the long, cold corridor leading to the kitchen. Lise had unplugged the one by the desk, flustered by its relentless ringing. She hadn't expected this much attention. She was content to be known by only a small circle of poetry enthusiasts who wrote her passionate, admiring letters, often scented and stuffed with violet petals. And she felt happy and flattered when she received notes from children impatiently awaiting the next Kim book. But never before had she experienced the dubious celebrity that sticks to a name and disregards the individual. For hours on end, hordes of people (curious, perverse, drunk and mad) had yelled into her ear as if it were a rubbish chute into which one dumped everything that couldn't otherwise be disposed of.

When I say Lise was flustered, I'm merely relaying Kurt's and Mrs Andersen's perception of her emotional state, because the only fair way of depicting a person – at least in this case – is through the impression she makes on others. My narrator doesn't like herself much. When she leaves faint, delicate traces in the minds of others, she makes note of it, then retreats as swiftly as a photographer who successfully captured her changeable face from a flattering angle. She is convinced that it is only possible to love her if you do not know her. She believes that if happy couples exist in this world, their happiness depends on a near-total ignorance of each other's true nature. Thus, every lover is deceived, and Vilhelm's hatred of her is completely understandable. It all began the moment she (like countless generations of women before her) took her marriage for granted, the way one takes breathing for granted. That's when the odalisque stumbled; that's when the frightened, fragile gazelle became a growling hyena. And the feeling of having behaved foolishly, exposed oneself irreversibly and lost face for good, grips Lise to such a degree that she (just like me) does not know how to go on living. I'm not asking you to love her, but she could really use some compassion. Anyone denied love in childhood will forever struggle to believe they are worthy of it. As for me, I intend to love her, now that I am freeing myself of her. Besides, at long last, she's being quite sincere. As she scribbles away, she too would like to know how the pathetic drama she's unfurling for the morning paper's fickle, scandal-hungry audience will end. And just as Kurt, with a polite but sullen air, opens the door to her study, she envisions Mille, and it occurs to her that this girl with the slow, warm hands and the deeply attentive gaze typical of all short-sighted people must know something crucial about the events that transpired, and which she may very well have set in motion.

'Mille's on the line. Would you like to speak to her?'

Standing in the doorway is the rag doll from Café Skovly by St John's Hospital, because Lise can never shake her first impression of others. She also cannot tell that people age over the years. Intellectually, she knows it, but her emotions do not comprehend it.

'Yes, Kurt. You can just hang up. I'll put the plug back in.'

Her heart pounds with panic, while a storm of unruly emotions threatens to overpower the investigator inside her. She smiles mildly into the empty room, but the smile is insincere.

'Hello, Mille. (Thank you for stealing him from me. How I

adore to suffer and grieve! Thank you for stuffing (that is, transforming) him and fattening him up like a castrato. I'm sure he has developed a wonderful soprano. No, no, I'm not bitter in the slightest, my dear. In fact, I'm just dying to understand the both of you.)'

'I'm glad you didn't hang up.'

'Now why would I do that? (Bravo, Lise! This is precisely the harmless voice she can't resist.) Of course, I've been cross with you, but you know it's not in my nature to hold a grudge.'

'I read your column today. It's brilliant. I'm already looking forward to the next instalment. But I'm calling because I want to have a chat about everything. I feel terrible about the silly letter I sent you. After all, you have no idea how it came about.'

'No, but I'd like to. You see, I was so horribly alone when the two of you disappeared. (And instead of swallowing those stupid pills that couldn't even kill an infant, I should have come over and dragged him right back, even if it meant throwing sulphuric acid in your face!)'

'I know, Lise. But actually, Tom kicked me out, and you'll think I'm raving mad, but I miss the boy terribly. You know, when a woman doesn't have children of her own . . .'

Then, the two twittering women were interrupted by a lunatic who had availed himself of the busy line. Breathlessly, he huffed:

'My name is John. I love you. Say something, anything! I can only get off on the voice of a famous woman.'

'Idiot,' said Lise politely, having suddenly slipped into another realm, bygone and unreal. 'You nearly scared the life out of my poor mother and me, standing there in the door to the pissoir with your pitiful crown jewels on show. It's your fault everything got so complicated afterwards – you realize that, don't you?'

'That's right, keep going, more, more, yes, here it comes . . .'

Lise hung up and pulled out the plug again. She thought:

Neither of us mentioned Vilhelm. She collected herself and called for her rag doll. (Oh, Lise, be careful, you learned contempt for others from Vilhelm. And before him, your mother, who was just a rung above the bottom herself, yet preached: 'Climb upwards! Life will always knock you back down.' But you couldn't help loving those who have nothing left to lose – the whores on the streets who offered you coffee and cake and always had pockets full of butterscotch, and the drunkard who slept in the cellar, the one your brother taught you not to fear. He was cold, so the two of you pinched your father's old, moth-eaten coat and laid it over him. And right then, you loved him ineffably, with an earnest, simple reverence for all God's creations, no matter their form, no matter how wretched their state.)

Kurt was not at his usual post, and she ran through the flat, calling his name until she found him in Vilhelm's room. He was sitting at the desk and hastily slammed the drawer shut, as though he had been caught snooping. The only thing Lise registered was that he was not gone, and she rushed over, knelt down and rested her head in his lap, her hair splaying across Vilhelm's trousers like so often before as she buried her face in the reassuring smell of man, of sex, something no soap could wash away. It was mingled with the sharp scent of anxiety, linked inextricably to it in some distant moment, and as her heart calmed, she inhaled deeply and cried:

'Oh, God, Vilhelm! Kurt! Never leave me again.'

Kurt watched this strange scene unfold as if from afar, like something he'd seen in a film or read in a book. He didn't move a muscle; he couldn't, though he had a vague sense that he ought to, at least, stroke her hair.

'I'm not leaving you. I was just bored of manning the phone.'

Lise got to her feet, blinked a few times and returned to reality.

'Sorry, I'm feeling a bit tired. Let's unplug both telephones, lest Mrs Andersen thinks this place has turned into a madhouse.'

Vilhelm's Room

They could hear her loud clattering in the kitchen – the only sign that she, too, had been thrown off kilter.

Lise avoided looking around the room, which she hadn't set foot in since before their stay in the summerhouse.

On the way out, she said in a perfectly neutral tone:

'I'd be very grateful if you could look up Mille's number for me. I seem to have forgotten it. Her last name is Bertelsen.'

Kurt promised, and once she had left, he opened Vilhelm's diary to a random page, as if searching for the verse of the day. As always, he found what he was looking for. It read: 'How will I ever escape this hell? Though my jealousy is worse than any imaginable physical pain, it alone binds me to her. Like Catullus says:

> *Now I know you: so, though I burn more fiercely,*
> *yet you're worth much less to me, and slighter.*
> *How is that, you ask? The pain of such love*
> *makes a lover love more, but like less.*

For all I care, Olesen can go on claiming she's only slept with that fat, pleb-loving shrink she'll likely never see again. There will be others, if only because I want there to be. After all, great pleasure and great pain go hand in hand. For her too, I believe. Why can I only love her vicariously? Through her poems, and when she isn't around, I feel an overwhelming need to shield her against this brutal world – though she will primarily suffer its brutality through me.'

Kurt closed the diary and felt a strange hum in his blood, the same anticipation as when he lay in Mr Thomsen's bed, listening to the old hag's depraved stories. In all that Vilhelm had written about Lise, Kurt only saw and relived the sublime, lost mornings he had spent upstairs.

Before he went out to look up Mille's number, he grabbed

a pen from the inner pocket of the jacket (Vilhelm's pen, Vilhelm's inner pocket) and wrote on one of the diary's empty ruled pages: 'It won't be long before I go upstairs and fetch my suitcase.' And as he wrote those words, he felt almost happy. He was certain she had neither alerted the civil registry office nor the police. But what would Tom do without him? Now his sympathy gathered around the boy with no future. A strange thought struck him regarding the boy's mother: If Vilhelm could manage to escape, Kurt could too. All of a sudden, he realized that fleeing was all he had ever done.

14

The day Lise had lunch with Mille, Tom went for a stroll on the ramparts with a girl one year younger than him. He had promised her his mother's autograph, for she was a romantic, sensitive girl who had read Lise's love poems and felt they perfectly echoed her own fears and yearnings. Since Tom had his father's surname, she had only recently found out who his mother was. But Tom had secretly been smitten with her for a long time, discussing her attributes with his friends in the coarse terms boys always use to save face. Lene was slightly taller than Tom and even skinnier than him, with long, blonde locks cascading down her back. They had started school the same year, and in first grade he had found her insufferable because she always cried over the smallest things, so her eyes were perpetually red and rabbitty. But soon they would be all grown up, and one day during lunch break, Lene had slipped a note into his hand: 'Want to go for a walk after school? Yours, Lene'. He had no idea how she had got the impression that she was his, having scarcely exchanged more than a handful of sentences with her over the years. And of those, most were spoken during the school play 'The Prince with the Cold Heart' because he hadn't wanted to kiss her.

She was wearing jeans and a lambskin-lined windbreaker. Tom's jacket was only padded with cotton wool, which was why he was shivering even though the weather was quite mild, considering Christmas was around the corner. Since Vilhelm's disappearance, Tom didn't like asking his mother for anything that required money. She never said no to him, but he worried they were becoming poor. Why else would they be moving to a smaller flat? There wouldn't be room for his father if he ever came back. And what about Kurt? He was wandering around with Vilhelm's passbook and all the hundred-kroner notes he found between the pages of those outdated textbooks; it amused Tom to no end that his father had never bothered to pick up his university diploma. There was no evidence proving he was who he claimed to be. It was like Kurt's certificates for his supposed half-finished law degree; if he were telling the truth, surely he would have fetched that suitcase of his by now. Tom had never spoken to his mother about Kurt. And he couldn't bring himself to betray Kurt's trust either.

The two children found themselves by Restaurant Ravelinen on Amager, and since Tom needed warming up, they ventured inside and ordered two cups of tea and white bread.

'I'd love to meet your mother,' Lene said, adding, 'you look just like her.'

'She's a nice lady,' Tom replied evasively.

At the moment he didn't feel like inviting a girl over. But he felt at ease in Lene's company. In fact, it had been a long time since he had felt this good. Unable to find the words to tell her, he mustered all his courage and placed his hand atop hers on the red-chequered tablecloth. It felt like a bird fluttering its wings briefly before settling. She smiled shyly. He grinned:

'My dad always says that if you ever feel like risking your life to rescue a girl from a burning building, you should immediately run away.'

'And do you?'

'Yes, like rescuing you. Not running away.'

★

Vilhelm's Room

Mille had reserved the café's private room so they could talk in peace. Really, she would have preferred to meet somewhere else, but Lise always insisted on visiting the scene of the crime. The two of them had often shared meals here with Vilhelm, and last time he had got so drunk he could barely sign the bill. 'I like you best, Mille,' he had said, 'but I feel a stronger connection to my dear little wife.' Had Lise intentionally worn her grey dress with the white collar and cuffs? She'd been wearing it that day too, but it could be a coincidence. Mille was sporting long green slacks and matching pumps with extremely high heels. She always managed to look stylish without spending a fortune. It was an example of what Vilhelm liked to call 'keeping a tight rein on things'. Both fell silent as the nosy old waiter they'd never liked poured their white wine and took Mille's order. For the sake of convenience, Lise asked for the same thing. She avoided Mille's eyes behind the clear lenses of her spectacles. Mille's gaze, much like Vilhelm's, was attentive and penetrating – a trait they shared, given their short-sightedness. Mille said:

'The letter I sent you was dictated by Vilhelm. He hated you so much he needed an outlet.'

'Does he still?' (Lise didn't actually care any more.)

'No, all he talks about is that great love of yours. It's not exactly what I'd expected.'

'The letters I wrote were dictated by Greta, a fellow patient. She was behind the advert too.'

'How close to the present do you intend to take your articles?'

'Not too close. Did Vilhelm ask you to ask me?'

'No, he doesn't know I'm with you. He thinks you hate me.'

'I used to, but now I can neither hate nor love anyone.'

The waiter returned, and as he fussed over their table for a suspiciously long time, they held their tongues.

Once he was gone, Lise pulled herself together and said:

'Why did he come to the luncheon with the publisher?'

'For your sake, Lise. He thought you'd have a hard time explaining his absence. You know how torn he was between us. He felt he had to make a choice, but couldn't. And when he came back to me looking unhinged but also deeply unhappy, I was packing to leave for my parents. Had he arrived ten minutes later, I would have been gone. Would you mind telling me what happened?'

'I wouldn't mind, but I can't explain it.'

'Just tell me how you experienced it, Lise. You see, he's never said a word about that afternoon.'

Her voice was gentle as she clasped her large hands beneath her chin, ready to listen. That was what made her irresistible, Lise thought; it was a rare gift in a world where everyone wanted to talk but few cared to listen. And there was something that needed to be taken care of before Christmas – a matter that would become easier the better she understood it.

As Lise spoke, she stared through the dusty blinds of the windows, so lost in thought she would scarcely have noticed had Mille been discreetly swapped out with another listener.

'It was a charming house, but a bit too small. The phone was in Tom's bedroom, which meant that he was constantly woken up by Vilhelm's incessant calls to you – about *Carmen*, Bizet and that maddening "Habanera" he couldn't get out of his head. It made me so furious I even suggested we invite you to visit, but he vehemently opposed any further contact between the two of us. As I'm sure you've heard, we brought along a young girl – Kirsten, her name was – to do the cooking and cleaning, but also because we were somehow no longer capable of being alone together without getting into fights so vicious they could have ended in murder. Kirsten was a student, twenty years old and very sweet, but Vilhelm behaved like a lecherous old goat, slapping her on the behind and that sort of nonsense. That day, after

Tom ran off, Vilhelm broke down in tears because "his only son had fled at the sight of him" and so on. Kirsten hurried into the kitchen and set a place for him at the table. He muttered a quick hello to the publisher and his wife before knocking back several shots of schnapps, then grabbed the first book he could reach without having to stand, which happened to be Karen Blixen's *Shadows on the Grass*. He's always had a knack for finding a suitable passage for any occasion. Blubbering, he began to read aloud: "Personally I have always had a predilection for boys, and have at times reflected that the stronger sex reaches its highest point of lovableness at the age of twelve to seventeen . . ."

'He got no further, and I would have liked a word with my publisher and his wife, who seemed rather taken aback, but there was no way to speak to them in private, and they weren't the sort to drown their discomfort in alcohol, unlike Vilhelm and so many others . . . Kirsten, who wasn't drinking either, offered to refill our glasses, but at least she had the sense to put on a record, and then Henrik (that's the publisher) and I danced, Vilhelm danced with his wife, but Vilhelm and I didn't speak or touch. You know how unsettling that can be, and the whole time I kept thinking that as long as they were there, nothing truly terrible could happen. But they were eager to leave and I don't know them well enough to have asked them to stay. And in any case, I'm sure dreadful rumours were already circulating about our situation. Then, suddenly, we were alone – Vilhelm and I and Kirsten. He could hardly stand upright but that didn't stop him from lunging at Kirsten, scaring her out of her wits so she fled to her room, which didn't have a lock, with Vilhelm right at her heels, but what was it to me? She wasn't a child. Nevertheless, I followed. Kirsten was screaming and thrashing under Vilhelm, who had her pinned by the wrists, and I became livid, clawing and scratching and biting him until he grabbed a suitcase, threw a few things into it and stormed out of the house, shouting, "You bourgeois bitch!" I watched him flag down a cab on Strandvejen, and I haven't seen him since.'

Lise delivered all this in a flat, monotone voice. She looked up at Mille in surprise, as though she had forgotten she was sitting there, then resumed nibbling at her shrimp cocktail. Mille raised her glass.

'Cheers,' she intoned gravely.

'Cheers.'

They both finished off their wine. Mille shook her smooth, black hair and said:

'John and Jette are to blame.'

'That doesn't surprise me. John has hated me ever since I based one of my characters on him.'

'They kept telling Vilhelm you'd ruined his career. They were the ones who introduced him to Helene, and really, from that moment on, your relationship was doomed.'

'But, my dear Mille, he did come back to me after her. Except then you came along, needing someone to pick lint off and scrub on the back.'

'He wasn't your property, Lise. And besides, you always felt best when you were in hospital. No man could put up with all those suicide attempts, especially since you never meant them seriously.'

Lise smiled at a pleat in the velvet drapes that separated the room from the rest of the café.

'No, never,' she said, almost cheerfully. 'And now you don't know what to do with your teddy bear, do you, Mille?'

'He's never loved anyone but you. That's all he talks about. I don't really exist to him.'

And this conversation was absurd, thought Mille, who, as it happened, had severed ties with her specialist doctor father just the other day. During a recent visit to her parents, Vilhelm had fuelled up on alcohol beforehand and hadn't held back at the table either. Her mother had valiantly attempted conversation but eventually gave up in the face of Vilhelm's incessant interruptions. When he left the room, her father had remarked: 'A classic case of Korsakoff syndrome. Alcohol-induced psychosis – send him packing, my girl.'

'The thing was,' said Mille, 'I was hopelessly in love with him. You know how charming and witty he could be when he wasn't too drunk.'

'And now?'

Lise buttered her slice of sourdough and unwrapped the Camembert.

'Now I take care of him, tending to him as one would a patient. Because that's what he is. I'm glad when he's well and gaining weight, things like that, and I do care for him. But I'm not in love any more. Things were better when there were three of us.'

'As far as I'm concerned, everything is great now,' said Lise, her mouth full of cheese and bread. 'I've grown so fond of Helene. Her disdain for me came from a good place. She wanted him all to herself, which was perfectly understandable. But you, with all your free-spiritedness, wanted to start some sort of commune and God knows what else. Maybe you even convinced yourself. But the love between him and me is such that one of us must now die . . .'

'Are you out of your mind, Lise?'

Mille stared at her in horror, but Vilhelm would have understood. He would have churned out some Kierkegaard: I don't begrudge time for being wicked, but for being passionless!

'No, just a little drunk. I'm not used to drinking any more. It's a bloody expensive vice . . .'

'Let me take care of the bill. I'm the one who invited you.'

'Too bad we don't have Vilhelm and his chequebook. We can't put this on the newspaper's tab, can we?'

'I never imagined you could be this way,' said Mille, her dark eyes glistening, 'After everything you and I have shared . . .'

You bitch, thought Lise happily, you chose him over me. Your big, doughy hand pushed mine away, but such things can't be discussed in broad daylight, and besides, I suddenly couldn't care less about you . . .

Her smile remained all the way home, though her victory was so bitter it might as well have been a defeat.

15

When Lise returned home, she found Kurt preparing one of the South American dishes he was so fond of making. He rarely had the chance to, as Mrs Andersen took it as an affront to her cooking. Today, however, was an exception. She had been in a rush to get home to Mr Andersen who had developed a crick in his neck, leaving his head stuck at an angle, as if his neck muscles were too short on one side.

Lise walked up to Kurt as he cleaned the mushrooms. Why was it a good thing that he was here? Her curiosity about him was purely professional, nothing more. He worked swiftly and skilfully with his hands. Perhaps he had once been a ship's cook, but it was easier not to know any specifics. She smiled at him and briefly rested her cheek against his shoulder. How about loving him, now that nothing else seemed to matter? She said: 'Where did you get the money for all this food?'

'From Vilhelm.' (He didn't look up from his chopping.) 'He hid banknotes inside his books. I've found eight hundred kroner. You can have what's left.'

Lise snorted with laughter: 'That doesn't surprise me one bit. I hid money from him too. If we really become poor, Kurt, we can start scouring my bookshelves too.'

The word 'we' made Kurt uncomfortable.

'Did you find out whether Vilhelm is coming back?' he inquired politely, finally glancing up at her.

'He's not coming back. Nor do I want him to.'

She turned and went to her bedroom. Here she took off her coat, hung it in the closet, then knelt in front of her dressing table and pulled out the bottom drawer. Her hand groped among underwear and towels until it found what it was looking for: a small black silk purse adorned with mother-of-pearl, borrowed from a friend years ago and never returned. She opened the clasp and withdrew a little brown pill bottle. There they were, wrapped in a newspaper clipping she had saved – a psychiatrist's warning to general practitioners about the potentially lethal effect of a sleeping aid commonly considered harmless when taken at just slightly higher doses. Lise had been able to obtain fifty of them easily, and ever since, it had been a comfort to hold the glass bottle in her hand. She had set a date for her death: the day Vilhelm left her for good. Lise had never intended to wait for a natural death, or as people liked to call it nowadays, a dignified end. In the last three years, she had lost her mother, her brother and her father. She had watched her mother calcify and grow increasingly helpless over the years until her heart gave in. They hadn't expected the old man, who was a decade older than their mother, to survive the loss. As it turned out, her death made no impression on him whatsoever.

But when Edvin, Lise's brother, succumbed to a horrible cancer, her father had broken down, lamenting that nothing was as awful as outliving one's own child. He was almost completely deaf, but even when he had been less hard of hearing, he and Lise had always found conversation to be a challenge. Now all he wanted was to die. He was ninety years old, and a few months later, he did. Although they had never been close, Lise felt that his death propelled her into the family's oldest generation. It was Edvin she missed, though. The two of them had always talked about their childhood, and now she was alone with it. There was no one left who could tell her things she couldn't remember from when they were children. She felt forsaken somehow, and she couldn't bear to visit her brother's family; everything in their home remained just as it had been when he was alive. When she told Kurt 'he's not coming back', she partly meant her brother, who loved life and would never have found joy in owning a little glass bottle of deadly pills.

Lise tore up the article and threw it in the wastepaper basket. Then she put back the pill bottle, but the image of it didn't leave her. As soon as she closed her eyes, instead of the usual darkness she saw a mesmerizing ballet of white pills and brown shards: pouring in, spilling out, flowing together in a rhythm so lovely and graceful, as if set to a Rococo melody. It was a shame she couldn't share it with anyone. She thought of Vilhelm's occult phase all those years ago. He had claimed that by photographing the retinas of murdered people, one could identify their killer. She no longer believed it to be impossible. With no one, however, can you share the most important things in life. She had already ascended to another level of existence where pure love is possible, and which few people ever reach. She was hungry and looking forward to the exotic mushroom dish. If only Vilhelm could see her now. How it used to upset him that she never sat down at the table in good spirits and with a healthy appetite, and to cheer him up she had said – on this, or some other occasion – that all good things were either fattening or immoral. He'd been amused by that. Oh, you enemies of Vilhelm (he boasts of being like the infamous politician Edvard Brandes, who prided himself on being the most hated man in Denmark), you should hear his laugh, those rare, unused noises from the depths of a woeful soul, a splashing cascade of sounds like the first rusty spurts from a newly repaired tap, suddenly pouring ecstatically over hands, shoulders, loins – for even in the moment of climax, this laughter gushed out of him and made us all giggle . . .

★

That evening, three people had a nice time together, or rather: Each of them had a nice time individually and therefore enjoyed each other's company. After his date with the girl, Tom's recent worries about not being like everyone else in one crucial way had been assuaged. Kurt had vague ideas of returning to Mr Thomsen's bed, to the darkness, the stench, the lust aroused by a liver-spotted bag of rattling bones; a pure, immaculate ugliness. Unconsciously, he had made his decision when Lise rested her cheek on his shoulder. The spot still burned, because he had grossly misinterpreted it as an invitation now that she had given up hope of Vilhelm's return. Lise looked at the two of them, radiant and full of affection, praising the food and telling them about the little drunk antiques dealer who had sold her the bronze candlesticks. He had demanded one hundred kroner apiece but ended up selling them for ten. She had bought them because Vilhelm had accused her of not having a good eye. He had a habit of plucking such pronouncements out of thin air, but they never missed their mark. A few days later, he claimed she only ever caught on to fashion trends ten years too late. She immediately sought the counsel of one of his first poppy-flower girls (she'd forgotten her name), who took her to a department store where they bought her a three-quarter-length coat with a fur trim at the neck, sleeves and hem, but Vilhelm's only remark was that it had been too expensive (though she had paid for it herself) and that he preferred women who had no interest in clothes and knew how to engage in intellectual conversation. After that, she wore her dressing gown all day long and read Simone de Beauvoir's *Letters to Sartre*.

These gruelling transformations were obvious to everyone except Vilhelm, who never thought twice about the things he said. When Helene came into his life, he declared that he found uncultured women with their heads full of vapid pop ditties completely irresistible, but at that time Lise was immersed in

Vilhelm's Room

the book that would earn her the Children's Book Prize from the Ministry of Culture, and Vilhelm had temporarily (though fatefully) slipped from her mind. All this she shared with her audience of two because it was so funny and so tragic – and, ultimately, it was her very life at stake, and the boy considered asking her whether he could invite Lene over for tea, and Kurt told her he used to love night-time strolls through Copenhagen, and she said: 'Why then, go for a walk, already! You shouldn't be cooped up like a cat – at least the cat is neutered!' She and Tom laughed, but Kurt grew solemn, put on Vilhelm's shearling coat and announced that she was right; he would take a walk on his own. Only a week ago, that prospect would have sent her into a panic, but now it was just fine, and when the door clicked shut behind him, she stared at her son with such fanatic adoration that the glare of it was reflected in his violet-blue eyes, and he smiled his sweet smile and said: 'Mum, I know a girl who'd like to meet you. I like her. Think she could visit sometime?' Oh, Tom, she thought, her chest tightening, you're no longer a child. Attach yourself to another woman and everything will be much easier – that which must now occur, that which is difficult for a little boy, but bearable for one who is almost grown. 'Yes, sweetheart. She can come by tomorrow. After school, at three o'clock, perhaps?'

And then, unexpectedly, it did hurt to see his joy; life was painful, living was not normal, after all, most people are dead – and my darling, she thought, I'm so tired, what a jolly time we've had tonight, haven't we? I'm off to bed, maybe there'll be something good on the TV. I really hope Kurt took the key with him – I don't know the day or hour, but it won't be long – I look forward to it the way one looks forward to those parties you'll soon be going to; one expects something to happen that will alter the course of one's life, because that's what it is to be young. One yearns to meet someone who's different from all the rest, and when one carries that expectation within, it's usually fulfilled by whoever comes along first. For the object of love, you see, is beside the point, one projects onto him the qualities one needs him to possess and on very rare occasions he will embody them, and then he will turn around and do precisely the same thing: see something in one that is not there – and that, my boy, is as close to love as we can get. A person's sex and age are not so important, for in this world one finds the oddest of couples. You were so amused by the story of the French mountain farmer who bequeathed his entire fortune to a thirteen-year-old sheep that was born lame! Instead of putting it down, he raised and cared for it, and they had a happy life together. He felt no connection to any other living being, and should his beloved sheep pass away before him, he would put a bullet in his head.

The love between your father and me, or the legend of it, which runs through your veins too, was probably no less strange. We took turns wishing the other would wake up ugly, crippled, afflicted with any physical disability whatsoever, anything to guarantee us security and lifelong protection against all those who threatened to come between us; jealous individuals of every sex and age who believed they could exploit whichever one of us was presently weaker – but they only tired themselves out, until eventually, something was taken too far, and what we had – and have – was scattered to the winds. Yet you are the son of two proletarians who owe nothing to anyone for what they've become. In our hearts lives an inviolable pride in having been given nothing from birth, but also resentment towards a world that crushed our parents. Your great-grandfather hanged himself in prison. Your grandmother was only four years old and never forgot the day the blue gendarmes came and took him away. I would have liked to have known him, no matter the heinous crime he may have committed. Like me, he carried death in his heart, and like me, he had decided on the day of his death – the day he lost his freedom. Just as I have no freedom left but one: the freedom to die when I please. And that is beautiful. One does not forfeit the right to die because one is a mother. Now I lie on the white solitude of the bed, and I reconcile myself with the whole world. I forgive it, I love it. Yes, even your father – I love him too, though I may never understand him . . .

16

A brown suede coat ambled through the rain-soaked streets, which were slippery and shiny like eels. The lining and lapels were covered in white shearling and it was slightly too short for Kurt; his head jutted out like a bird peering over the edge of its nest. Though he was not one to dwell on things, he did find it odd that Vilhelm had left behind all his possessions (including his wife and child) as if he had merely stepped out to post a letter. In some dark way, he admired it. He walked the way he imagined Vilhelm walked – hurriedly, slightly hunched, rushing from a lover's tryst to an important editorial meeting at the office. While Mr Thomsen's clothes had been rags devoid of personality, Vilhelm's were those of a living human being; their smell of man, sweat and tobacco was strong and good and impossible to remove, regardless of how often they'd likely been washed. And because Kurt was angry with Lise and the boy for laughing at him, the coat carried a trace of that anger too, mingling with Vilhelm's own, as expressed in his diaries: 'I want to see her suffer even more. Yet it's impossible to bring her to her knees, because for her, suffering is so easily transformed into pleasure.'

It is Vilhelm's Lise who now occupies Kurt's thoughts, not the real Lise, whom he hasn't for a moment perceived. There were few evening strollers in the city centre, and like Kurt, those who passed him had no particular destination. By eight o'clock, most

Vilhelm's Room

people are sitting in front of the TV, or they're at the theatre or cinema, or having dinner with friends or family. Anything is possible, except aimlessly wandering the cold November streets, not knowing where chance will lead them. The only exception is young couples in love; one never knows what they might get up to. The rest are lonely souls, predominantly men, and they look like figures in the background of a painting, placed there to give the scene a touch of life. They seem to belong, as if they had sprouted from the cobblestones themselves, feeding on the damp of the brick walls. Kurt stood out solely by virtue of his elegant dress. Like the others, he felt drawn to the bars, and plenty of new ones had opened up while he was leading his mole-like existence on the Boulevard. He was looking for a quiet spot, free from loud music or slot machines, and for the first time since his return from America, he wanted to get very drunk. The desire was partly Vilhelm's. It seeped through his clothes: his words, and the palpable longing he had left in those two people who only seemed truly happy when they reminisced about the violent outbursts he was prone to after drinking twice as much whisky as any normal man could handle. Kurt tried to remember the millionaire heiress in California with whom he had shared that transcendental encounter. Perhaps he was the father of a six-year-old child. It was of no significance to Kurt. He was not fond of children. Besides, she had presumably taken care of the matter, and his fear of the civil registry office was likely unfounded. Though he had forgotten all about the incident, it might still have given him a certain pleasure he subconsciously was seeking again.

Vilhelm's coat billowed like a sail when the wind swept around the street corners and caught hold of it. And though the legs beneath it belonged to Kurt (the Indecisive), they carried him to The Drop Inn, in whose cloakroom the coat had hung so often during those five years when Vilhelm was obsessed with Helene. A particularly strong gust flung Kurt towards the swinging doors, and as he handed the coat to the cloakroom attendant, he was reminded of the plaster cast of Queen Nefertiti standing on the windowsill in Vilhelm's room. It had been a gift from Mrs Carlsen, the proprietor of The Drop Inn, and Lise had remarked that Vilhelm's lovers were always giving him things; gifts that mostly proved useless since what they needed most at home were kitchen utensils. From Vilhelm's diaries: 'How can it be that the woman I would die for now fills my ears with nothing but her household predicaments?' Dated 1958, back when Lise cooked and shopped and kept a household book that Vilhelm reviewed every evening, underlining all the expenses he deemed unnecessary with a red pencil. His relationship with Mrs Carlsen had been brief and fleeting, but she had fiercely protected his and Helene's affair. They were always given the most discreet corner table, and from her spot behind the bar, she would watch their enraptured faces with motherly affection as they sat with their legs entwined under the table and their hands clasped tightly as if fearing they'd be pulled apart and sent back to their respective places. Mrs Carlsen had been Mille's predecessor. Convinced that Vilhelm needed to be freed from his marriage at any cost, she resigned herself to the fact that she could not be the one to save him.

As there were no other tables available, Kurt joined two men engrossed in a lively discussion. He politely asked if they minded, but they paid him no notice. When the waiter placed a whisky on the rocks in front of him, however, he sensed someone observing him intently. Turning halfway in his seat, he found himself looking into two large, grey eyes framed by pitch-black lashes and painted-on brows. The rest of the face had a bluish, ghostly pallor, lit up from below by a lamp with a red silk shade, which accentuated a tendency towards a double chin. The young woman smiled invitingly at Kurt, who recognized her but could not recall from where.

He finished his drink and, with a dim sensation of obeying someone else's will, strode over quite uncharacteristically and sat down across from the heavily made-up girl. The girl continued to smile as she called to the hostess behind the bar:

'Elise, how about a round on the house?'

Mrs Carlsen personally brought them two drinks and winked at the girl like a brothel madam:

'Look at his clothes,' she chuckled, 'don't they look familiar?'

The girl didn't reply but went on smiling at Kurt like a doll with a wind-up key in its back.

'How come you're wearing Vilhelm's clothes?' she finally asked, and in that instant he recognized her as the girl with the gouged-out eyes from the photograph.

'I live in his room,' he informed her, 'I sleep in his bed and wear his clothes . . .'

'And are you also sleeping with his wife?' Helene asked breathlessly, flushing so brightly it showed through her white face powder.

'Yes,' lied Kurt, who couldn't remember the last time he had done so.

'Does Vilhelm know?'

'No. I don't know him and have never met him.'

'Isn't she a little old for you? Though, from what I've heard, Vilhelm doesn't only go for fresh meat these days either.'

'Lise Mundus is a great and famous lady.' (He didn't know why he was defending her when, just this evening, her fame had driven him out of the flat; all those people on the phone and at the door, all those photos of her face splashed across newsstands, and yet, somewhere deep inside, he understood it – her inhuman loneliness.)

'She's frigid and perverse. She has no idea what it means to love,' Helene exclaimed so loudly and forcefully it drew glances from the other guests.

'Why do you hate her?' he asked with surprise, distractedly chugging down everything Mrs Carlsen set in front of them. 'She doesn't own him any more. He'll never go back to her.'

'Because I love him. For the six months they were separated, we were happy. But then she sent him the right letters and the right pictures at the right times. He cried his eyes out over her "brilliant prose" and put a photo of their son on our bedside table, and when I finally got pregnant, it wasn't his. Now the child is with my parents, and all I want is to win Vilhelm back.'

Helene continued to stare at Kurt, who still looked exceptionally handsome when one imagined him without clothes. Trim, broad-shouldered, with skin like heavy silk. Helene felt that she was alive again, and that this life was fantastic. Mrs Carlsen came over to join them, big and warm like a brooding hen – and just a little devious.

'Vilhelm's clothes don't suit him,' she said, grinning.

'They don't suit Vilhelm, either,' Helene retorted. 'They're from his time at the foreign ministry. These days, I hear he wears a blue chore jacket and chequered trousers to the office, in solidarity with his workers.'

Involuntarily, Kurt hooked his thumbs into the armholes of his waistcoat like the boy had taught him, and the two women couldn't help but laugh.

'He's a catch,' said Mrs Carlsen. 'He'll prove quite useful, if you're smart about it.'

The remark was superfluous. A muddle of emotions flooded Helene's soul, hazy plans whirling around in her whisky-soaked brain. She told Kurt that she was a hairdresser and a model, then invited him back to her room on Vester Voldgade; she hadn't terminated the lease when she moved in with Vilhelm.

Kurt's soul also drifted in clouds of whisky. He thought of the photograph of the naked Helene, her eyes gouged out by Lise; he thought of Lise and the boy, who had compared him to a neutered cat. And he thought of Vilhelm's anger – and of those who had raised him to make something of himself, to become a politician, perhaps, in a world he did not suit, just as Helene didn't. Then music began to blare and Helene sang in a soft, clear tone about love and roses, and suddenly everyone around them was adorned with white garlands and something impelled him onwards, into a plotline that belonged to someone else, and he knew it, yet he did not . . .

The telephone rang at Vilhelm's office. It was almost midnight, and outside his door he heard the festive hubbub that always accompanied the paper being put to bed. Like behind the scenes before a premiere, he thought, except the paper premiered every day. The front page lay on his desk: '19-Year-Old Masseuse Murdered'. A Frenchwoman, so they had only managed to dig up a lousy amateur photograph of her. He stated his name into the receiver and yawned loudly when he heard the low drone of Helene's voice.

'You'll never guess who I just slept with.' Strange that she hadn't realized their little game had long since ended.

'No. The prime minister, like the last time?'

'No, my darling. This time I was mounted by your wife's lover.'

'That's a lie. She doesn't have one.' He leant forwards in the chair, tugging at his collar with his free hand as if he couldn't stand the feel of it against his neck, irritated by this sign of his own arousal.

Helene laughed. 'Oh yes, she does. A handsome young fellow. He's living in your room and wearing your clothes. Care to hear the details?'

His heartbeat quickened, and he licked his dry, thin lips. 'I can be there in half an hour. You're home, aren't you?'

'Yes.'

Triumphant, Helene hung up. She was standing in the phone booth outside her front entrance. Kurt had been sent home. Their rendezvous had been rather confounding, and though it hadn't paid off in and of itself, she knew it would lure in Vilhelm, despite his being immune to these particular temptations as of late. The last one had been the prime minister, just before Easter. That time, Vilhelm had planned to see Mille, and on top of that, he was supposed to spend time with Lise and the boy at that summerhouse he actually detested, because Lise, on the advice of some friends he'd never particularly liked, had built it during the six months she'd been alone with the boy. Amidst all these mutually exclusive plans he had abruptly taken off with Helene to a hotel in Vejle, where he had loved her for five days straight, insisting all the while that he had to get over this obsession which had nothing whatsoever to do with love. He assured Mille and Lise of this too, and at a dinner at Søpavillonen they had both ranted about that witch Helene who resorted to such crude tactics.

It was mad, and yet Helene couldn't forget the five years of her life – from the ages of nineteen to twenty-four – when she had seen Vilhelm or spoken to him on the phone every day. Her father owned a country inn on the island of Funen and until she moved in with Vilhelm, he had sent her a thousand kroner each month for her studies, which were as airy in nature as Kurt's. Her parents did not know that she had moved out of John and Jette's place when they began to have misgivings about the relationship they themselves had helped orchestrate. Nor did her parents know that she worked at a hair salon without proper training and had a side gig as a model. They were proud she had completed gymnasium and, in their ignorance, assumed she must be studying something or other at university. When she and Vilhelm moved in together, her parents had invited the odd couple to their flat above the inn, where they ate roast turkey and drank cordial the colour of red wine because her mother was taking disulfiram. Fortunately, Vilhelm had brought his hip flask. The old folks (who were Vilhelm's age) promptly cut off her monthly allowance, which was unfortunate, as Vilhelm wasn't particularly inclined to support her for the rest of her life. Make-up alone cost a fortune. With great artistry she applied her mask, without which she had a round, plain face; a fact she was painfully aware of. Had it not been for the protective layer of make-up, Lise's fingernails would also have left more lasting marks.

She opened the door for Vilhelm, stark naked, her face caked in make-up, but everything was not as it used to be. It was Kurt, not Helene, he wanted to hear all about, and he became furious with Kurt, because Lise belonged to him, Vilhelm, and in her desperation and naivety she had fallen into the clutches of this swindler who was only after her money. And it was madness, all of it, and he didn't know what he was doing with Mille, and he didn't know why he had despised Lise so much that he couldn't stand the sight of her, because clearly she couldn't survive without him. And now he, too, was set in motion; he would return to his little wife and their son. But not quite yet – first he would await her next article, because it was so outrageously brazen of her to expose their relationship in such a public manner. The whole thing made him laugh, with big tears rolling down his cheeks, and why on earth, one might ask, was he leading a terrible smear campaign in the paper against authors who lived off the taxpayer's hard-earned money when he now sobbed to Helene: 'Why doesn't Denmark prize its poets? No one thinks of them while they're alive, and no one notices when they die.'

After leaving Helene's, he hailed a taxi on Vester Voldgade, and as it drove past his old room, he noticed the lights were on behind the curtains. He thought of everything he had left behind and resolved to return to Lise and the boy, whose fates rested in the hands of a dubious young man who without a doubt was not featured in *Who's Who*. The murder of the masseuse on Rådhusstræde came to mind, for it was precisely among parasites like this fellow that her killer would be found.

17

It isn't necessary to know everything that goes on in the ripples spreading from Lise's big decision. From now on, I will tell you only what I feel like telling you, save for a few remarks which I will mention in passing, like a tour guide mechanically reciting key facts about notable landmarks for the umpteenth time as weary tourists hurry by, eager to return home and recount it all.

For instance, the barmy Mrs Thomsen once again calls Mr Andersen to report that she saw Kurt lurking near the masseuse's flat on the very same evening she was murdered. The detective inspector, still plagued by the crick in his neck, sloppily scribbles something on a notepad and silently wishes his wife would stop working for those nutcases. It worries her that Tom has invited a girl over for tea and that his mother seemed pleased about it. He's still a child, Mrs Andersen had told her husband, who agreed against his better judgement, knowing that if the boy were ever to fall in love, she would truly feel unneeded – and then who would she sacrifice herself for? The boy and the girl could visit, and Andersen could offer them the sort of fatherly advice he might have given his own son, had he had one. In his opinion, Vilhelm is a cad, not because he left his wife (who, frankly, could put up with her?), but because he abandoned his son. Andersen has searched in vain for Kurt's records and knows that, officially, he does not exist. That, however, is none of his business. He does feel some pity for the poor sod, given that the old hag has taken to reporting him for all manner of sex crimes, to such a degree that if Kurt really were guilty of murder, no one would believe it. While he jots down the details of Vilhelm's coat and the legs underneath it, an original idea strikes him: He will insinuate to his wife that Kurt could be the murderer. Surely then she'll finally tire of catering to this fellow at the expense of the lady of the house.

But he can spare himself the worry, for on that night Kurt unwittingly went up one flight of stairs too many and had no time to wonder why the key didn't fit before Mrs Thomsen opened the door and wordlessly led him to his old spot under Mr Thomsen's naphthalene duvet. There, beside the headboard, stood the suitcase filled with glossy business cards, American paperwork detailing mysterious repayment plans and student loan applications addressed to a university in Boston, alongside a stack of polite rejection letters and the irrefutable evidence of a half-finished degree from the Faculty of Law in Copenhagen. When Kurt finally woke up, he felt an indescribable sense of relief, like waking from a terrible nightmare. He retreated into the familiar comfort found in the absence of change, and there we shall leave him, wishing him a Merry Christmas or some equally insipid pleasantry, which is nevertheless better than nothing. Having served his purpose in this book, he now falls out of its pages like a bouquet of dried violets, colourless and without scent.

But Kurt lives on in Tom's heart as he explains to Lene (for lack of words to describe what really happened) how Kurt helped him and his mother through a very tough time. What more does my reader need to know? After all, we are growing tired of each other and could use a little diversion so as to meet again with light hearts. Or heavy hearts, since the reader I am writing for is greatly saddened. He – for it is a man – mourns the fact that Lise now has no other option but to die her gentle, happy death. He cares for her, though often enough she has driven him up the wall. But anyone who saw her in those days when she was filled with her impending death can attest that she seemed to relish life once fear had left her soul. She even began to love the world again, but only because it would be annihilated with her.

Her publisher called: 'We're very interested in the articles about your marriage, and we'd like to publish them as a book.' Be my guest, poor friend, who must go on living after I'm gone. They'll likely ask you for a quote on the occasion of my death, on the radio, in the papers or on TV, and you'll say many clever things, for you couldn't help but care for me a little. Yet at the luncheon, you retreated with your wife because you didn't want to get involved – that was the last time you saw me with Vilhelm, and didn't that just make the whole visit worth your while? Nevertheless, I love you, because, scared as you are, you can only survive by believing all conventional feelings are true. Long ago someone or something deceived you too, for it is not inconceivable that you were once a child. That's the biggest difference between people. In most cases, the child inside them is dead; betrayed and abandoned, it never shines through the creases and wrinkles of the adult face bestowed on them – a face which seems to bear no resemblance to the original, however that came to pass.

But in the case of Lise and Vilhelm, my two rather unheroic heroes, their childhood faces can still be discerned, making them easily recognizable to those who haven't seen them since. Also Mille wears the face of an aged child. Because Vilhelm always goes on about Lise's long, lustrous locks, she has grown her smooth black hair to her shoulders, only to be informed that he prefers tomboys – short-haired, flat-chested, with deep, husky voices. But this tactic simply doesn't work on Mille, and that's one of the many reasons he's tiring of her. Vilhelm requires a constant challenge in life, a perpetual inner state of tension, like a soldier who sleeps with his boots on, not knowing from which front to expect the next attack. Lise had satisfied this impossible need in the first few years of their relationship, when he had incessantly fought for her survival and well-being, but after her desire for stimulants had quieted, their evenings took on a strange emptiness which could only be filled by heated arguments over the household budget, meals or a missing shirt button. Later, the challenges came from the outside in the form of enticing job offers (he has yet to be employed anywhere for more than five years), each accompanied by a set of highly demanding tasks that, from one day to the next, would bore him endlessly. And when Vilhelm is bored, he becomes dangerous, a trait he shares with many others.

Lise did not know, or did not consider, that he could not stand to be alone. And she had the habit of admitting herself to hospital, because the role of patient satisfied so many of her infantile needs. But she shouldn't have done so during the Christmas of 1965. That time, she fell under the spell of an old doctor who prescribed her narcotics as if they were sweets, and when that became untenable, she confided in Højborg, who immediately had her committed to rehab. Vilhelm had been distraught. It was like the time she went to Russia: as if he had been abandoned by his own mother and didn't know when she'd be back. Everyone at the office felt sorry for him, and John and Jette invited him over for dinner to help him through Lise's absence – and to introduce him to John's young cousin, who had recently moved in to ease her parents' concerns about her living away from home. John and Vilhelm would often frequent Kakadu Bar to pick up exotic dancers, and therefore John knew that the overly made-up, doll-like Helene, with all her bouncy youth and nascent decay, would be just the thing for Vilhelm, now that he was feeling down because his wife had lost her marbles. It's curious to think how much cruelty seemingly harmless people are capable of when merely presented with the right opportunity. John wholeheartedly wished great pain and suffering upon Lise because she had modelled one of the villains in her children's books after him. He might have tolerated her giving the character a 'receding chin', but the fact that he was also a chess master made it far too obvious. His wife agreed, and what's more, she found it utterly disgraceful that Lise forced her husband to sleep in a room no bigger than a storage closet, especially considering his social standing.

In short, they wanted to stir the pot but never imagined that Vilhelm's relationship with John's cousin would become so serious. Nor did Vilhelm, who in recent years had tried to overcome his all-consuming sexual appetite by any means necessary. One such means had been Mille, along with Lise, who proved too old and tired; at least that's what he realized that summer when jealousy seized him and he could no longer bear the thought of his two women having anything to do with each other. An extremely complicated love life was part of his self-image, but suddenly he found himself alone with Mille, whom no one else desired, and who wanted him all to herself, this Florence Nightingale with the dark, ingenuous eyes – and God, how boring it was. And now that a handsome young man was sleeping with Lise (which he hadn't thought possible since he had stopped loving her), the old robber knight awoke in him once more, but this time she would not be an easy conquest.

Even if Lise had been aware (as I am) of all this in those days, it would not have changed her plan in any way. Only in the early years with Vilhelm had she been as happy as she was now with death, and she had no intention of letting that happiness go again. She had tea with Tom and his first girlfriend. Big blue eyes and a mop of bright blonde hair atop a tall, rounded child's forehead. The similarities were so striking that it couldn't go unnoted.

'She looks like you, Mum,' Tom noted, 'back when you and Dad were happy.' And it was true; Lise fetched the photograph taken at Himmelbjerget, and the girl decided that Tom resembled his father most, and Lise agreed and found herself telling the girl about the time when Vilhelm bought a car for twenty-five-thousand kroner. This was not long before they moved to Copenhagen. He had just got his licence, and when the car had been delivered and stood parked in the garage, he kept running outside to check that everything was as it should be. It wasn't, he claimed; there should have been a clock on the dashboard. He called the salesman, who told him he was mistaken. Then, Vilhelm had said, almost sheepishly (and it was both a curse and a blessing that she remembered such things): 'You see, Lise, I've never owned such a big, shiny, expensive, new thing! I mean, I never could have imagined that I'd come so far.'

And she told the listening girl how moved she had been, for she too couldn't believe how far she had come and could never shake the feeling that one day she would be exposed as a working-class wretch who had wormed her way into circles where she didn't belong. And the girl told her how much her mother had always admired Lise, and now she did too, and Lise couldn't help but laugh, remarking that before long, children would be telling her how their grandmothers loved her poems and read the Kim books aloud to their grandchildren or great-grandchildren – and it was a very enjoyable afternoon, and it would never happen again, because what made it enjoyable was precisely that it was happening for the last time.

One evening, when she had forgotten to unplug the telephone, it rang. It was the frightening old lady upstairs:

'No need to go looking for Kurt,' she rasped triumphantly. 'He's with me, and that's where he'll stay.'

Then the receiver was replaced with a soft click, and it turned out there was still something that could hurt, not too much, but enough for the time to draw closer. There was no longer life in Vilhelm's room, and soon there would be no room either. If she could not hold onto Kurt the Failure, she could not hold onto anything any more. Perhaps she might have managed if Tom hadn't invited Lene over. He had most likely discussed it with Kurt, who was doomed to be the third wheel in every relationship, except upstairs with his macabre lover. And so we approach the ending, like tired children trudging home in the falling darkness after their evening escapades. And Vilhelm decides to await the publication of the remaining articles, which have, of course, already been written because Lise is conscientious to the end. He will wait for them at Mille's, in the large living room with the low furniture and dim lighting. As he rambles on about all his years with Lise – about happiness, madness and a pathological weakness for dangerous pleasures – he eagerly awaits the Saturday edition of the rival newspaper, annoyed that Hairfair probably bought the series for a song because Lise doesn't know her own worth, and had it been possible, he tells Mille, he would have liked to publish the articles himself, but after leaving her as he did, her pride wouldn't have allowed it.

And Mille, who is crocheting a shawl for her mother (it's exasperating, thinks Vilhelm, that her hands are never still), asks if his pride is also preventing him from calling Lise? He says yes, and it's partially true. He has always been so afraid of rejection that he has never asked anyone for even the smallest favour in his entire life. By which I mean he has never asked a man, because he expects women (such as his secretary, for instance) to make his life easier in all practical matters without him having to ask. Although it's ridiculous (but of course, the ridiculous and the tragic are not so dissimilar), he would never have left Lise had she 'kept a tight rein on things'; if she had made sure that the shirts and towels were in their proper places so he wouldn't have to scramble around searching for them when he was in a rush; if she had known how to prepare food in an enticing manner and give the vast, empty flat that female touch which made it a home and not just some kind of stable where one slept and ate.

In theory, he had some respect for feminists, which now counted all his female employees, but heaven forbid he should ever have to live under the same roof as one. Meanwhile, out of the corner of his eye, he noticed that Mille too had changed. The living room smelled of rancid flower water, and the books he took from the shelves now piled up on the nightstand because she no longer put them back in their place. When he came home at night with John or the managing editor, she was impossible to wake, and they had to scrounge the kitchen for food and drink themselves. More importantly, he had lived out his complicated passions for so long that the simplicity and intimacy of living with just one woman no longer held the slightest appeal. Vilhelm the Faithful (said without a trace of irony) intends to return to his little wife, awaiting only a strategically opportune moment. And Mille the Redeemer, who knows that Lise is unhappy, intends to give Vilhelm back to her and takes quiet, diligent steps towards this end. Yet it all comes magnificently too late, because Lise is an artist preparing her life's greatest work, hovering between Heaven and Earth like a star dangling from a silver thread . . .

18

Reading through the preceding chapters, I now realize that I may have at one point implied that Kurt would become a murderer. For such ends, however, I have made him far too stubborn and wilful to be used for anything that does not benefit or please him. He didn't even want to stick around until the end of the book, a common risk for writers like me. That's why I could never write for the theatre. I tried when I was a child, believing I would one day master every genre. Suddenly all my characters would be crowded on stage when I only needed two of them, and they couldn't very well turn to the audience and excuse themselves with an 'I'll be off then!' or something equally idiotic. Moreover, I am unable to account for the psyche of a murderer as I lack those ingredients in my own mind. And though Kurt the Forgetful will sometimes drown certain anxieties in alcohol, he most definitely cannot summon a murderer's rage and passion. My Vilhelm, on the other hand, could, and it's not improbable that he fled our home to avoid becoming a murderer. Lise is shocked by this revelation about Vilhelm's character, which she has uncovered with my help. If people do not fear him, he fears them. And who wouldn't prefer the former? How a relationship begins determines its entire course.

In the beginning, I feared him because he fought my addiction with utter ruthlessness. He reported the doctors who supplied me with pills to the medical council, which led to one of them losing their licence. When he actually succeeded – when my love for him won over the urge for blissful self-destruction and my soul unfurled in joy at this miracle – he rushed home from work, saw the glow radiating from me and asked, 'What have you taken?' He wanted a confession, but there was none, and after that I was no longer a challenge for him to rise to. Yet my fear persisted and merged with the fear of my mother. A fear of words. 'You're too ugly to come to the dance at Folkets Hus.' And Vilhelm: 'A man whose wife doesn't clean her fingernails will never make a career for himself.' Perhaps I only grow attached to people I fear, while for my Vilhelm, the opposite was true. Mrs Andersen did not fear him, and he paid her the most exquisite attention. Our boy did not fear him, which led Vilhelm to fear that he might tell others what was going on at home.

There's a funny story to this. When the boy was eight or nine, he titled a notebook: 'Childhood Memories'. On the first page, in neat cursive, it read: 'Chapter 1. I was born on (insert date) at Usserød Hospital. My parents were very strange.' With that, his memoirs began and ended, as if all the strangeness had simply overwhelmed him. And now, Lise no longer fears Vilhelm. She fears no one and nothing. Life can only inflict a dull ache, like the faint discomfort one feels at the dentist when numbed with laughing gas. She receives alarming notices from the tax authorities (and now Kurt is no longer there to 'make an arrangement' with them), what mad times these are, and she thinks: Society. Just like in her ever-present childhood, she imagines it as an infinite grey plane full of cavities where people hop around barefoot over something resembling lava. The holes are oases that swallow up those who have jobs, while at the edges, bitter battles are fought, the victors of which slip into the holes too. It appears they are determined to bankrupt her. Bills in window envelopes addressed to Vilhelm fall through the mail slot, but she doesn't forward them. He probably has obligations to her of some kind, but neither of them will ever file for divorce. It's far too much of a hassle, and Vilhelm won't even go to the barber any more but instead has Mille trim the iron-grey hair at the back of his neck. Their relationship is one of equal dependency, like between an angry, helpless infant and his mother who can't bear his cries. Reciprocal fear – that is something he has not yet experienced. He says: 'A nest without chicks is empty', and thinks of his son. But immediately, Mille starts to cry, and her big tears are perfect teardrops, while Lise's crying gives her rabbit eyes and lashes . . .

It was a mild winter, and usually Lise didn't care about the weather, but today she did. She doesn't know much about what she is going to attempt, but one thing is certain: She does not want to freeze. Because she's serious this time, it has to happen far away from people, so no one can intervene and rescue her, thwart her beautiful, carefully crafted plan. Up to this point, everything and everyone seem to be aligning towards its completion, yet some mishap could still get in the way. She thinks of the jokes about people who make the long trek to Grib Forest, find the most secluded spot, and just when they're about to hang themselves from a good, sturdy branch – along comes a scout troop, ready to do their good deed for the day.

One day, the two negotiators stopped by, looking very humble and contrite, and it isn't unthinkable that they may have pitied her a little now that Kurt was gone, but this was their job, after all, and they spoke very loudly and slowly, for Lise had gone deaf to their voices, like a child so absorbed in a game that her name must be called several times before she reluctantly returns to reality. They asked her to vacate the premises just after the 1st of January, since the old widower had been allocated his flat earlier than expected. She acquiesced with a smile, and once again their powers of persuasion went unexercised. They concluded that the date was of no importance to her; she must have been paid so handsomely for the exposés that she could buy a house and never set foot in the widower's old flat. She forgot them as soon as she closed the door behind them. She forgot everyone, even the boy, if they weren't right in front of her. She never thought of Vilhelm any more. She didn't think of how it must have felt for him to read about their marriage; it was all the same to her. She retreated into herself, like a heavy object sinking to the bottom of a barrel. There they were, all her dearly departed whom she loved so fiercely.

Lise had only seriously attempted to take her own life once before. She had been twelve years old at the time. Her mother, who didn't love Lise, had accused her of stealing a twenty-five-øre coin from her purse, which had been left unattended on the kitchen table for a moment. No matter what Lise said, she couldn't convince her mother that she hadn't taken it. The amount was unaccounted for in the household book, and it was taken for granted that her older brother would never steal. In her despair, she had denied the accusation again and again, bawling as she yelled (for her mother always brandished melodramatic, proverb-like religious phrases, which were part of the spell she cast): 'May my arm wither and fall off if I'm not speaking the truth!' And in the narrow kitchen between the sink and the stove, her mother had screamed: 'That's it, I'm leaving! If you don't cough up the money, I'm never coming back!' And the situation had been so grave that her mother hadn't even slapped her as she usually did whenever given the chance, and because her father was unemployed, it was an enormous sum, and it was hard enough to account for every five-øre in the household book, let alone explain the absence of a whole twenty-five-øre. You could buy a block of liver paté for that, or five bags of day-old bread, or even something as frivolous as a beer. And the

Vilhelm's Room

money never turned up, and the suspicion clung to Lise forever, indelible and without mercy. Young Lise could not bear it.

She waited for a day when she was home alone, but her mother only left the flat when absolutely necessary. However, as luck would have it, she developed a toothache, and when it hadn't subsided after a week, she set off for the public dentist to have the tooth pulled. At this point, I must add that Lise was the most well-behaved, obedient child one could imagine. She was, to her mother's regret, not pretty, so she did her best to compensate in every other area. She became uncomplicated: a girl who never caused trouble, who received decent marks in school and never drew any complaints; someone who wanted to please others, hoping in vain to be loved. Meanwhile, her brother (who likely stole the twenty-five-øre) was loved without much effort on his part. He was a boy, undeniably beautiful and talented, and he excelled in woodworking and sports. But that day, when Lise was finally home alone, she felt almost as happy as she does now. The attempt failed only due to her poor knowledge of anatomy. She stabbed the bread knife into her wrist where she presumed the artery to be, and the blood flowed thickly and steadily as she lay on the floor with a pillow under her head, imagining how her sobbing mother would throw herself over her dead body, ruing the day she accused Lise so unjustly. But death did not come, not even a little. She squeezed at the wound with her thumb and forefinger, but nothing else happened. Her mother returned, bleeding from the wound in her gums, and asked why she was sprawled out like that, making such a scene. A few days later, Lise had to be taken to the doctor after all because she had hit a nerve, leaving four of her five fingertips numb to this day, which, as it turns out, is not such a great loss. When Vilhelm suspected her of having taken something every time she was in a good mood, she repeated the procedure, though only half-heartedly. It became a way of escaping herself, which most people achieve through a good night's sleep – something Lise had never known. Her insomnia was, so to speak, congenital.

How she tires me, and the reader too; that much is clear. Be that as it may, on the 19th of November, she gathered her passbook, her perplexing tax documents and the lease agreement and ventured to the bank with the lot of it. Normally, she's scared to death of banks and post offices; she feels herded from one counter to the next, from one suspicious, dismissive face to the next, and in the end, she doesn't know which way is up or down. But she is no fool, and on this day, she plays the whole 'my husband always takes care of such things' part, though her pride usually forbids it. She is the picture of utter confusion: her hair is dishevelled, her stockings have runs, her voice cracks like an adolescent boy's and her trembling hands fumble in the depths of her purse as she asks for the bank manager. No one else will do. And since she is, in reality (which concerns her less and less), a highly esteemed customer, he appears, slick and smiling and somewhat curious, for he too has been following her series with avid interest. He leads her to his enormous office, offers her a chair and a cigarette and is, as intended, swayed by her blatant helplessness. There is no need to worry, he assures her. As he reels off numbers and dates, her head spins, trying desperately to understand, but she can't, and when he realizes this, he smiles and says: 'You and your son can live comfortably for the next few months and after that, you can simply come to us for a loan.' When she looks stunned, he adds that no doubt she has 'something in the works', and wouldn't her publisher be delighted to pay her an advance? He is a jovial man who approaches the issue with good humour. He doesn't know how seriously Lise takes her situation, and that while she loves to make fun of others, she doesn't understand when people make fun of her. 'Comfortably for the next few months'

Vilhelm's Room

is all she takes away from the conversation, and she really hopes Tom's siblings will support him, hopes it mechanically, and is so overwhelmed with joy at what is finally within reach that she feels like singing and dancing all the way home; as if her all-too-recognizable face didn't already attract enough attention.

The next day was a Friday. Mrs Andersen, who had never let her down in fifteen years, called to say she would have to stay home because her husband couldn't move his head due to gout, and she wanted to be there when the doctor visited. She told Lise to cook Tom's egg in a pot of cold water brought to the boil and left to simmer for one minute, and hoped her husband would be well enough for her to be back at work the next day. Lise didn't see such things as a coincidence but as a sign from God that he approved of her plan and wouldn't stand in her way. She made breakfast for herself and the boy, who laughed because she was always injuring herself in the kitchen. This time, she had burned her finger while pouring water from the egg pot, and he told her about the anti-Christmas sentiment in his class, and as far as he was concerned, they could skip the Christmas tree altogether, and Lise could see him only faintly through the ballet of brown glasses and white pills behind her eyes. Although their hands were very close, she avoided touching him, the orphan, and he said: 'Cheerio!' as he left, and imagine if they could have held a joyous farewell party, but he wouldn't lack for anything since her book sales would now pick up again: 'Now we wish to buy you, woman! / All the sweetest words, / all the most precious words shall be yours, / woman, though you cannot understand, / now everyone wishes to buy you / with all the most precious words.' It was Tom Kristensen's elegy to a parachutist, and now he was dead too. On the day of his death, Lise appeared on Swedish television, and in Malmö, the journalists, puzzled by her grief, had asked: 'Who was Tom Kristensen?'

It was pouring rain, but surely it would let up eventually. In the meantime, she packed the yellow pigskin leather bag she had bought in Paris with an uncharacteristic meticulousness. Apart from the bottle of pills, the bag contained two half-litre cartons of milk as well as two fizzy drinks to ensure she had enough fluids, two beer glasses in case one broke, a pack of cigarettes, a big box of matches and a torch in case she unexpectedly found herself in the dark. She placed a napkin between the bottles so they wouldn't clink. Her usual purse contained everything she always carried, and she saw no reason to remove any of it: a few lipsticks, a powder compact, a small, smudged mirror and a wallet with several hundred-kroner notes she couldn't be bothered to count. The problem was Tom's sleeping bag. The zipper was broken, and its cover was missing. Since the biggest impediment might be the cold, she had no choice but to roll it up and tuck it under her arm as if it were perfectly normal to be carrying around a sleeping bag. She laughed merrily at the thought. She planned to set off as soon as the rain stopped, and definitely before the boy was let out of school.

Restless, as if everything were ready for guests who won't arrive for hours, she wanders through the rooms, drifting through the long, dark hallway with walls the colour of old mustard, into the kitchen, which reminds her of those children's drawings where one must spot five differences, into the maid's room, cluttered with discarded toys and removal boxes full of wood shavings; and back again through the three grand parquet-floored sitting rooms, where she curls up for the last time in her corner of the Nielaus sofa whose arms the cat has completely shredded. It's not worth re-upholstering until the little sharp-clawed creature is dead. She smiles at the thought that the cat will outlive her, gently stroking its shiny brown fur, for it has been trailing after her all this time and now lies there, front paws tucked, fixing her with its bright blue stare, intense

Vilhelm's Room

and expressionless. She looks out at the naked trees along the edge of the bike path. It's raining more softly now, a gentle patter she has always loved. Back home on her childhood street, it always used to rain; in her memory, it rains so tenderly and sadly. She brushes her fingertips against her face, and it occurs to her that she should cover it to avoid being recognized, like when she would wear fancy dress during Carnival as a child. Nothing in the world is as wonderful as hiding in plain sight and being alone. The blessing of anonymity.

She will tuck her hair into the old woollen hat she knitted in therapy during one of her hospital stays and has never worn since. And she will hail a taxi and ask to be driven to a specific street in Hillerød, which she knows borders the forest. The rest will be easy. She only needs two hours of peace and quiet, and she knows that after taking these pills, one stays put and doesn't wander around in a daze, unlike barbiturates, which will make a person get up to all sorts. For the first time in a long while, she thinks of Vilhelm, who would be proud of her for once. How many times has he begged her, enraged and desperate, to 'just get on with it', and he was right, and where in the world has the time gone? Soon, the boy will come home from school, perhaps with Lene, his surrogate mother, and in her heart she has already returned this morning's 'cheerio'. And then, the following happens: Disguised in a raincoat, rubber boots and a hair-stuffed hat, sleeping bag under one arm, yellow bag under the other, and her suede purse over her shoulder, happily prepared to meet her certain death, she must pass the door to Vilhelm's room, in which no one has set foot since Kurt left. At that moment, something inside her mind breaks, the door seems to open all by itself and she is swept inside, already freed from the burden of her body. She collapses onto the bed, clinging to an ice-cold duvet, overwhelmed by the most tender, brutal memories – and the wall is stained with pain and despair, and she hears the telephone ringing and ringing, and she doesn't need to answer to know that it's him. She stands up, adjusts her hat, gathers all her bags and closes the front door with a quiet thud, the very last sound of her lived life.

Vilhelm hung up the telephone, his face haggard and pale with fear like that of a dying man. After the last article, he had no choice but to return to her. His complete indifference to Mille meant he was unaware of how deeply she shared this desire. If Lise died, it would be the end of him. At the same time, he hated playing God and intervening in the serious decisions of others. He had just wrapped up one meeting and was waiting for the next; the endless trade union negotiations, each dragging on with tedious monotony. If he owned the paper, he had told Mille, he'd have shut the whole thing down a long time ago if people insisted on making such a bloody fuss. And if Lise died, he would write her obituary himself. 'The world breaks everyone,' he would begin, citing a Hemingway quote he couldn't summon in its entirety – something about how it kills the good and brave first and takes its time with the rest of us. But perhaps it wasn't too late. He ordered a taxi and rushed downstairs, neglecting to tell his secretary when he would return. The delivery boy at the reception looked up in surprise as he left. And as the taxi pulled up, Lise headed for her death in another taxi or hired car, the details hardly matter. And Vilhelm kept pressing the buzzer until, at last, he removed his finger from the button. 'Holy Mother of God,' he muttered and wanted to fall to his knees. Then he heard a strange rattling behind him, followed by a raspy, sneering voice which said:

'You can spare yourself the trouble. Once they start running off to the woods, it's serious.'

'Yes,' he said to the old hag. 'This time it's serious.' And he made the sign of the cross, pleading to God for forgiveness because he would not report her missing . . . The rain was now bucketing down and would quickly freeze her unconscious body. Vilhelm headed back towards Rådhuspladsen, stocky and grey-haired, condemned to go on living – gripped by the fear of committing a mortal sin.

Down the street, a boy with long silky hair strolled home with his arm draped around a girl's slender shoulders. He hoped his mother would be as happy and affectionate as she had been ever since Kurt moved out . . .